Wanderlust

AN UMBER BLUFFS STORY

TÉ RUSS

For my Readers

Synopsis

Suffering from a bad case of writer's block, Peyton takes a 'glamping' trip to Noir Cove in Umber Bluffs in search for inspiration.

She finds all that and more when she meets resort owner Maverick Porter.

Chapter One

PEYTON

Kyra moaned wantonly as Gerard pushed her legs open wide, and then…

And then…

I let out a loud groan as I furiously hit ctrl+z on my keyboard and watched the words disappear.

Out of frustration, I selected everything in my document and hit delete.

Because it was all shit.

Now here I sat at my desk, staring at a blank page, the little cursor blinking tauntingly at me.

I blew out a breath, and let my head fall back, my eyes shutting closed. I could feel the sting of tears building up behind my eyes but I refused to let them fall.

This had been the same thing that happened every time I sat down to try to write for the last several months.

I would get up early in the morning, grab my coffee, read the daily scripture and then meditate. Then I'd open my document and…

Nothing.

Sure I'd get some words out, but nothing felt right.

And then I'd end up picking up my phone and scrolling aimlessly on social media to try to ignore the fact that another day had gone by, and I had nothing to show for it in my writing.

I admired my fellow authors who would make posts saying they weren't claiming to have writer's block, calling it writer's distractions instead.

But as for me...

My shit was blocked.

My muse had packed her bags and hit me with the deuces and taken the fuck off to parts unknown.

Cause I sure as shit had no clue where she was.

And I was desperate to get her back so I could get my groove back.

Conceding to another day of defeat, I slammed my laptop shut, blew out the candle on my desk and got up to leave my office.

Just as I arrived in my kitchen, my phone rang. I smiled when I looked at my phone and saw the picture of my best friend, Bianca, on my screen.

"Hello Miss Executive Producer," I chirped.

"Hello Miss Best Selling Author," she replied, causing me to roll my eyes.

"Once upon a time," I grumbled.

"Uh oh," Bianca said, her smile turning from a playful one to an empathetic one. "No luck again today?"

"No," I said, propping my phone up on the island. I turned to open the fridge in search for food.

"It's going to be okay babe," Bianca assured me.

I loved my best friend's optimism. But optimism didn't pay the bills.

And while my royalties were still decent and I had a

good little nest egg, I knew the money wouldn't keep rolling in if I didn't keep putting in the work and releasing books.

"Hey," Bianca said, forcing me to turn back to look at her on my phone. "Get dressed. Meet me at Enigma for brunch."

"*Beee*," I whined. "I'm really not in the mood to get dressed and go out today. I just wanna stay home and be a gremlin."

"Fuck that," Bianca said. "Get dressed. Meet me at Enigma. You need mimosas. Expeditiously."

I started to argue again, but Bianca cut me off. "I will come over there and drag your ass out if I have to."

I knew all too well that Bianca was not bluffing. She'd done it before and she'd do it again. For someone so tiny the woman was freakishly strong.

"Fine," I spat out.

"See you soon," Bianca sang and then hung up the video call before I could say anything else.

Giving up on finding food, I headed for my bedroom to find something to wear to my impromptu brunch date with my best friend.

I took a shower – hoping the scalding hot water would singe off the funk I was in from another unproductive morning – and then did my hair and makeup.

Once I was dressed, I looked at myself in the mirror.

I looked way better than I currently felt, I thought, running my hands down the bellbottom jeans that hugged my ass perfectly.

I grabbed my purse and keys, left my house and headed for my car.

"Hey Peyton!"

I turned and smiled at my older neighbor Mrs. Lee.

"Good morning, Mrs. Lee."

"Girl I had a pair of jeans like that some fifty years ago!" Mrs. Lee shouted.

"And I bet you looked good as hell in 'em," I shouted back.

"Shole did!" she cackled. "Wish I had a lil more hips and ass like you, but we get what we get. Unless we add to it."

Her words made me laugh out loud. "I heard that! I'll see you later, Mrs. Lee."

"Bye baby! Come by later, I've another pound cake for you."

She knew I couldn't resist her pound cakes. Mrs. Lee had run a bakery before retiring after her husband passed away. Now she just made cakes for the neighbors.

I grinned as I slid into my car and started it, already eager to get back to get a slice or three of her irresistible dessert.

Mrs. Lee definitely had a way of brightening my day.

I made the short drive through Ebony Hills to the other side of the city to Enigma.

I pulled up to the front of the restaurant and a valet driver hurried to my side of the car and opened the door for me.

"Miss Baker," he said, grinning at me, his eyes roaming the entire length of my body.

"Alonso," I replied back, sliding a tip in his hand. "Take care of my baby."

"Always," Alonso said with a flirtatious wink.

I shook my head and made my way into the restaurant.

I looked around and found Bianca waiting at our usual spot.

"Hey girl," I said, sliding into the booth on the other side of her.

"Hey," Bianca replied.

I studied her for a moment, and then looked down at the menu as I teasingly said, "Girl, did Cole blow your back out before you got here, because you are *definitely* rocking a post-coital glow, mama."

Bianca shook her head, her cheeks heating with a blush.

"Well...yes, but...that's not the only reason for the glow."

I looked up to find my best friend staring at me, her eyes sparkling with excitement.

My eyes widened as I dropped my menu.

"Bee! Are you..."

Bianca nodded, her eyes glittering with tears and we both let out a squeal, garnering attention from the other patrons.

But we were too excited to care.

I shot out of my seat and went to pull Bianca into a tight hug.

"Congratulations, Mommy!" I said. I pulled out of our embrace and placed a hand on her belly that was still flat and showing no signs of her pregnancy yet. "I can't wait to meet my lil godbaby."

"Hey ladies," Kiana, one of our favorite waitresses said.

"Hey," I said to Kiana as we both sat back down. "Sorry for causing a commotion. Bee here just told me some amazing news."

"Well congratulations on whatever news it is," Kiana said. "Can I start y'all off with some celebratory mimosas?"

"I'll definitely take one," I said.

"Just sparkling water for me," Bianca said.

"Got it," Kiana said with a nod. "I'll have those right out for y'all."

After Kiana left to get our drinks, I turned my focus back to Bianca.

"How far along are you? Is Cole excited?"

"I'm almost two months in and Cole is over the moon," Bianca gushed. "I can't believe it happened so quickly."

Bianca and Cole had only been married for a few months.

"I can believe it. Y'all stay fuckin' like rabbits."

"Pey!" Bianca said, but couldn't wipe the silly grin off of her face.

"Am I lying?" I argued.

Before Bianca could respond, Kiana had returned with our drinks.

"Do y'all want the usual?" she asked us.

I said yes, but Bianca shook her head, placing her hand on her stomach.

"I can't seem to keep it down these days," she said, a pout on her face.

She ordered something different and after Kiana left again, I reached over and gently patted her hand.

"It'll all be worth it when you get to cuddle your little bundle of joy in about seven months."

"I know," Bianca said, her smile returning to her face.

I held up my glass to Bianca and she did the same.

"To my niece or nephew!"

We clinked our glasses and both took a sip.

We sat and chatted about all things baby until our food arrived.

I dug in and after a few minutes of comfortable silence I could feel her eyes on me. I looked up, still chewing my food as Bianca said, "So, we're just not gonna talk about it?"

"I thought we were here to celebrate my godchild."

"We're here for that too," Bianca said, as she put down her knife and fork and folded her hands together on top of the table. "Pey...what's up?"

"That's just it," I said, dropping my own utensils in frustration, causing them to clang loudly on my plate. "I... don't know what's up."

"You've experience writer's block before," Bianca pointed out. "And you always bounce back."

"This...feels different, Bee."

"How?"

"I...it just does. I can't explain it. I just feel...empty."

This time Bianca was the one reaching across the table to pat my hand empathetically.

"You *always* bounce back," she repeated with even more conviction. "This time will be no different. It might be taking a little longer, but when the muse comes back you will be unstoppable, as usual."

She pulled her hand away and reached into her purse. "I have something for you."

My brows furrowed in curiosity when she passed me an envelope.

"What is this?" I asked.

"Open it and find out," Bianca said.

I opened up the envelope and pulled out the piece of paper.

As I read it, my eyebrows shot up. I looked up at Bianca, who was grinning at me.

"Figured you could use a little getaway," she said.

My mouth dropped open and I once again looked at the printout for a voucher for five nights at Noir Cove.

Noir Cove was a black-owned resort in Umber Bluffs, a town a couple hours away from Ebony Hills.

Bianca had visited for the first time a few years ago during the holidays with Cole when they ended up stranded in Umber Bluffs thanks to a snow storm. They'd gone back a few months ago for their honeymoon.

Bianca knew that a luxury glamping trip was on my bucket list of things to do and had told me how Noir Cove was the perfect spot, but I hadn't gotten around to making plans to go.

But now it seemed like my best friend had gone and made plans for me.

"Are you serious?" I said, feeling my eyes fill with tears. "Bee...this is so unnecessary."

"I beg to differ," Bianca said. "I think a change of scenery is *exactly* what you need right now. And I told you before...there's something magical about that place. Maybe going there...being out in nature and shit will help get those creative juices flowing."

"Like...my own little writer's retreat," I murmured quietly as I looked at the voucher again.

"Yes!" Bianca said excitedly. "Go! Become one with nature or whatever and get your mojo back, girl!"

I grinned, looking up at my best friend again.

"Thanks, Bee."

Bianca winked at me and we went back to eating.

I steered our conversation back to Bianca and the baby, but in my mind I was already trying to figure out what I should pack and when I should make my reservation.

Chapter Two

PEYTON

I got out of my car, slinging my laptop bag over my shoulder and angrily slammed the door.

As I marched up the walkway to my front door, the sound of Mrs. Lee calling out to me, made me stop.

"Girl, what's got you pouting like that?" Mrs. Lee asked. "Bad date?"

As usual, her words made me laugh out loud.

"No ma'am. Bad writing session."

"Sounds like you could use a slice of cake."

I didn't have to be told twice and immediately turned and headed over to Mrs. Lee's house. By the time I got over there she was already in the house and on her way to her kitchen.

I went inside and looked around, taking a deep breath in. Her house always felt warm and welcoming.

"So," Mrs. Lee said as she cut two large slices of cake. "Still no luck in the writing department, huh?"

"No," I said, picking up the fork and stabbing it into

the cake. I shoved the large piece in my mouth and chewed on the decadent dessert before I spoke again. "I *thought* a change of scenery would help, but no dice."

"Change of scenery..." Mrs. Lee repeated. "Didn't you say Bianca gave you a voucher for that resort up north? What was it called?"

"Noir Cove," I answered. "Yes, she did."

"So why haven't you went yet?" Mrs. Lee asked. "*That* sounds like the kind of change of scenery you need."

"It's...I don't know. Five days sounds like a lot."

"And what you got holding you here for five days?" Mrs. Lee asked, tucking her fist against her hip. "No writing...no man...not even a plant."

"Well just twist the knife even deeper, Mrs. Lee," I said, taking another bite of my cake.

But she was right.

It had been several weeks since Bianca had given me the voucher and I'd been stalling on making the reservation for no real good reason. And Bianca had been hounding me damn near every day asking if I'd booked a reservation yet, even going so far as to threaten to do it herself if I didn't hurry up and do it soon.

"I'm just saying...nothing is holding you here, sugah," she said. "Book the damn trip. Go to Noir Cove. Eat. Pray. Find you a sexy mountain man and ride him into the sunset."

Her last words made me choke on the piece of cake in my mouth.

As I continued coughing and wheezing, Mrs. Lee slid a glass of milk over to me, a sly grin on her face.

"Mrs. Lee!" I said, when I could finally speak again.

"What?" Mrs. Lee replied, feigning innocence as she dug her fork into her own slice of cake. "Good dick makes for good inspiration, honey."

She winked at me as she ate her piece of cake.

I shook my head. "Mrs. Lee, you are wild, woman."

"You don't know the half of it," she said. "Peyton?"

"Yes?"

"Book the trip."

I thought about our talk. She was right. There was no good reason for me to have put the trip off for so long. And I couldn't even remember the last time I'd taken a vacation.

So I pulled out my phone and found the email Bianca had forwarded to me that included the voucher for Noir Cove and clicked on the link to book the next available five days.

"Wow..."

I looked around in awe of my surroundings as I drove through the property of Noir Cove. Taking in the lush landscape all around me, I was low-key kicking myself for not coming sooner.

I was surprised by how just the drive alone had calmed me so much already.

Even driving through the quaint downtown area of Umber Bluffs filled me with a cozy feeling.

Eventually I pulled up to the main lodge of the resort. I parked my car, got out and went inside the building.

I made my way over to the reception desk and was greeted by two women.

"Hello," the first woman said. "Checking in?"

"Yes, I am," I replied. "Peyton Baker."

"Welcome, Peyton. I'm Monica Porter, one of the owners of Noir Cove."

"Oh! Nice to meet you!" I said, reaching my hand out to her.

Monica reached out and shook my hand and then looked over my shoulders, her eyes going wide.

"I'm so sorry," she said, quickly pulling her hand away before rushing from behind the desk. "Please excuse me. Sandra will get you squared away!"

I turned and watched as Monica began calling out to a group of men carrying stacks of chairs.

"No! Those are going to…"

I turned my attention back to the receptionist, Sandra, who was still smiling at me.

"We've got a wedding this weekend," she explained. "Miss Porter's brother."

"Ahhh, now the urgency makes sense," I said with a nod.

"Yep, he's finally off the market. Such a shame," Sandra sighed wistfully.

I grinned at the starry look in Sandra's eyes, and she blinked and shook her head. "I'm sorry about that," she giggled. "Can you give me your name again?"

"Peyton Baker," I said, and watched as she began typing my name into the computer.

"Yes! We have you down for a five-night stay in The Amani Suite, one of our luxe geodesic domes. We put you in one on the other side of the lake since quite a few guests here this coming weekend will be here for the wedding. It's quieter over there."

"I appreciate that, thank you," I said.

"Not a problem," Sandra replied. "Plus the views of the mountains on that side of the property are some of the best. Would you prefer to drive yourself or have a shuttle take you? They run twenty-four hours, so you can call anytime you need a ride back somewhere around the resort."

"Really? Wow! I had no clue," I said, pleasantly surprised. "I guess I'll take the shuttle."

"Of course." Sandra picked up the phone and after a moment she said, "Hey Daniel? We have a guest that needs a shuttle ride over to the north side…The Amani suite… yep…thank you." She hung up the phone and then slid a keycard envelope over to me. "Your ride to your tent will be here in a few minutes."

"Thank you so much, Sandra."

"Absolutely! And if you need anything during your stay, don't hesitate to give us a call."

I nodded, grabbed my suitcase and made my way outside to wait for my ride.

A few minutes later, a golf cart pulled up and stopped in front of me.

A handsome young man smiled at me. "Are you waiting for a ride to the Amani Suite?"

"That would be me," I said, reaching for my bag at the same time the young man started to climb out of the cart.

"I can get that miss," he insisted.

"Oh no, it's…fine…"

All the air left out of my lungs as I stared at a strong, mahogany brown hand wrap around the handle of my suitcase. My gaze traveled up to a thick, veiny forearm, and up to a bulging bicep that flexed as it lifted my bag.

"Here," a deep, velvety timbre said, causing my entire body to vibrate with awareness. "Lemme get this for you."

I stood, transfixed, as I watch the truest definition of 'tall, dark and handsome' carry my suitcase over to the golf cart and gingerly place it on the rack on the back of the vehicle.

And then he turned his gorgeous gaze on me and his

mouth curved up into a warm smile that heated my insides.

He held his hand out to me, as he continued smiling. "Miss?"

Like a magnet, my hand went into his and a zing of awareness, shot through my entire body as he helped me into the golf cart.

"Th-thank you," I stammered after I was seated in the vehicle.

"Of course," he replied. He turned his attention to the driver. "Daniel, take good care of our beautiful guest, aight?"

"Yessir, Mr. Porter," Daniel said.

'Mr. Porter' turned his heated gaze back onto me. "Enjoy your stay," he said, before turning to head inside the lodge.

The golf cart jerked as it took off and I blinked out of my lust-filled stupor.

Damn he was fine, I thought to myself as we rode along the gravel road to my luxury dome tent.

Out of nowhere, Mrs. Lee's words came barreling back to the forefront of my mind.

Find you a sexy mountain man and ride him into the sunset.

I tried to remind myself that I wasn't on this trip to find some dick. I was here to find inspiration.

Good dick makes for good inspiration...

The woman's words just wouldn't get out of my head, I thought with an amused grin.

The grin slid away when I remembered that Daniel had referred to him as 'Mr. Porter'. That meant he had to be the brother of Monica's that Sandra had mentioned.

The brother that was getting married this weekend.

Now it made sense why Sandra was so disappointed that he was no longer on the market.

Hell, now even I felt a bit disappointed, as my mind drifted back to how attractive he was.

"Is this your first time visiting Noir Cove?" Daniel asked.

"Yes, it is," I replied, thankful for the distraction.

We chatted for the rest of the drive, and I took in the beautiful scenery around me.

I'd seen pictures that Bianca had sent me from her trips to Noir Cove as well as the pictures on the resort's website. Despite those pictures being amazing, they still didn't do justice to quite how breathtaking this place was.

I'd never considered myself an outdoorsy girl. In fact, I was quite the opposite. I hated bugs, I didn't care for hiking through nature or any shit like that.

But after falling down the rabbit hole on social media of black girls in nature, I found the idea of it intriguing and wanted to experience it for myself.

A few minutes later, Daniel pulled up to a large, dome-shaped tent, surrounded by a spacious porch.

"Here we are," he said, parking the golf cart.

"Wow!" I said, staring up at the dome in awe.

By the time I got out of the golf cart, Daniel had already grabbed my bags from out of the back and was carrying them up to the porch. I pulled out my keycard as I walked up the steps to the door.

"I don't know why I didn't expect these to have locks," I murmured more to myself than anything, but clearly Daniel had heard me.

"Oh yeah, we take your security seriously up here," he said, as he stepped aside so I could unlock the door. "There are even locks for our regular glamping tents."

"That's good to know," I said, as I swiped the keycard against the reader. Once the little red light switched to green and I heard the locks disengage, I opened the door and walked inside.

"Wow," I said again, looking around the dome.

I watched as Daniel sat my bags down in front of the large king-sized bed that was in the middle of the room. On the right side of the room, just a few feet away from the bed was a round hydro-tub. Further off to that side of the room was a surprisingly large shower, and double vanity sink.

"The toilet is over there," Daniel said, pointing to the door on the left side of the room. There was also a small kitchenette as well as a sofa on the left side of the room.

"Our shuttle service is open twenty-four hours," Daniel said, capturing my attention once again. "And we also have room service if you don't feel like going back up to the lodge for food. Just give us a call."

"Thank you so much, Daniel," I said, reaching into my purse. I handed him a tip, and he tilted his head my way in thanks.

"Enjoy your stay," he said, before turning to leave, shutting the door behind him.

Once he was gone, I did a full circle, taking in the room once again. I turned and walked over to the large curtains next to the door and whipped them open. They were thick and heavy, I'm sure to help with the insulation even though the rooms also included air and heat.

Once I got them open, I stood in front of the see through portion of the dome, staring in amazement. The sun shimmered on the water of the lake. It was a great view from anywhere in the tent, and already I was imagining taking a late-night soak in the hydro-tub while staring up at the stars once it got dark. And waking up to the sight of the lake and mountains right in front of me had me eager for morning.

I hadn't even settled in yet and already I was feeling more relaxed than I'd been in ages.

I pulled out my phone and started taking pics and videos of the dome tent. I immediately sent them to Bianca.

BIANCA

Wow! That is gorgeous! 😊

I know right?! This place is unbelievable. Thanks again for this.

BIANCA

Girl, no thanks needed. Relax and have a good time. Send lots of pics and videos.

Will do. Love u.

BIANCA

Love u.

I put my phone down, rolled my suitcase over to the sofa and placed my laptop bag down on the coffee table. I kicked off my shoes as I took off my jacket and dove into the bed. As my body sank into the fluffy duvet cover, my eyes instantly grew heavy.

I tried to think about when I wanted to make another attempt at writing, but before I could fully even formulate my next thought, I'd dozed off.

When I finally woke up, several hours had passed.

I yawned and stretched my arms over my head. My gaze drifted to the view outside and once again, I was stunned at the sight in front of me. I rested on my elbows as I stared out at the sun setting behind the lake.

I got out of bed and decided to explore the small but cozy dome and truly check everything out.

I was pleasantly surprised when I opened the mini fridge and found a complimentary bottle of wine chilling. I immediately snatched it up, grabbed a wine glass and poured myself a generous amount. As I took a slow sip, I turned around to take in the dome again.

My eyes landed on the hydro-tub once again, and I decided it was time to go for a dip. I went and turned on the tub and while it was filling up, I dug my swimsuit out of my suitcase and then went to put it on in the bathroom.

By the time I came out of the bathroom, the tub was nearly full.

I turned the water off and was about to get in when I decided that it was time to snap some pics. I found my tripod and my wireless remote for my phone and got everything set up exactly the way I wanted it.

I grabbed my glass of wine and went to get into the tub. I let out a sigh as I sank down into the hot water, the jets jostling the water all around. Once I was set up the way I wanted to be, I started snapping pics of myself with the wireless remote.

After I'd taken quite a few shots in a different few poses, I tossed the remote over onto the bed, shifted so I could see outside the dome and grabbed my wine. I called out to my phone and commanded it to start playing my lo-fi mix on my music streaming app and sank even deeper into the tub to enjoy watching the sunset.

I didn't think about writing – or the lack thereof – or my self-imposed deadlines.

All I did, for the first time in way too long, was sit back, relax and enjoy the peaceful view.

Chapter Three

MAVERICK

"And now the caterer just isn't answering and I'm freaking the fuck out...Mav..."

My sister's voice barely registered in my brain as I sat staring at my phone, transfixed by the woman I'd met earlier in the day. I'd seen her as soon as she'd come out of the lodge with her luggage and found myself walking over to her.

She'd been stunning with that wild curly hair framing her pretty chocolate brown face. I couldn't stop thinking about those full kissable lips that had smiled softly at me when I helped her with her bags and into the golf cart before she'd been whisked away.

Once she was gone, I tried putting her out of my head. We had so many guests here at Noir Cove at any given time and with me being so busy around the resort that the odds of me seeing her again weren't non-existent, but definitely slim.

And then my phone had pinged, alerting me that someone had tagged the resort in a post on social media.

My dick had instantly sprung to life when I saw the picture she'd posted of her sitting in the tub in what I instantly recognized as the Amani dome tent. Her back was facing the camera, and the side profile of her face was angled so that she was coyly looking over her shoulder.

After staring at the picture for another moment, my gaze drifted down to the caption.

> PeytonB143: "On the hunt to find the muse, came out to nature to see if she's somewhere out here...@NoirCoveResort"

The muse? I wondered to myself as I liked the post and then clicked on her profile and began scrolling. It didn't take me long to discover that she was apparently a romance author. And then I found myself exploring her page which was filled with so much content.

"*Maverick!*"

My sister's voice finally made me snap out of my ogling.

I blinked and looked up at my sister, who was glaring at me.

"Sorry Mon," I apologized, shutting off my phone. "The caterer?"

"Canceled!" Monica said and began to fill me in on all of the details. "Mav, Mason and Tatum's wedding is this weekend, and we have *no* caterer."

"We'll figure it out, Monica," I assured her, as I pulled my phone back out. I unlocked it and our gorgeous guest's face appeared on my screen again and I was once again lost in the sight of her beautiful dark brown, almond shaped eyes, pointy nose and high cheekbones.

"How?" Monica asked, snatching me back to reality.

"I...don't know," I admitted, turning off my phone and shoving it into my pocket so I could give my sister my full attention.

Monica had been helping Tatum and Mason planned their wedding and she'd been on top of everything. She was a drill sergeant with heart, which meant she was always polite but she ain't take no shit and could get down and dirty if the occasion deemed it so.

But as the week of the wedding had arrived, Monica had become a bit more...high strung as the final preparations for the event began to fall into place. Or in the case of the caterer...fall apart.

"Have you told Mason and Tatum?" I asked.

"Are you crazy?" Mon asked. "They don't need the stress of this."

I nodded and stood. "Don't worry," I said. "I'll make some calls."

"Me too," Monica said, picking up her phone. I turned and left out of my sister's office and blew out a breath.

Finding a caterer in such a short amount of time to handle a wedding this big was going to be tough. I knew that just as much as Monica. But one of us had to keep a level head, and while Monica was usually that person, it seemed I was going to have to step up and take on that role.

I knew all my sister wanted was for our brother's wedding to be perfect. Mason had been in love with Tatum for a long time before he'd finally won her over the Christmas before last. Last Christmas he'd proposed and here we were just six short months later heading into their summer wedding.

I also knew Monica's emotions were all over the place because the anniversary of our mother's passing was quickly approaching. Although it had been several years at this point, all three of us still had a hard time dealing with this time of year, as well as around Thanksgiving since our father had passed away during that time in the same year that we'd lost our mother.

We all understood that he'd died from a broken heart. We knew he'd tried his best to stick around for our sake's, but…being without our mother was just too hard for him.

Monica had thrown herself into working even harder at Noir Cove to cope. Mason had taken off on a journey of self-discovery or some shit by traveling for about a year. And as for me…

I got lost between the legs of every beautiful woman that would willingly open them up for me.

The idea of finding a love so strong…so transcending like what my parents had was something I'd refused to even think of trying to find. I'd convinced myself that there was no way I was going to tie myself to someone so fully and completely.

After many therapy sessions though, I'd shifted my perspective on things.

Now, that love that my parents shared was a love my siblings and I all aspired to have.

Mason was the first to find it with Tatum.

And I'd be damned if I let a fucking caterer ruin the day that we all got to share in that would celebrate the union of my brother and his bride.

I had to get to work to help my sister fix this potential disaster, I thought to myself as I made my way through the lodge over to the lobby bar.

I needed a drink.

As I slid onto a bar stool, I pulled my phone out of my pocket. I unlocked it and was greeted by the alluring smile of PeytonB143.

"Evening, Mr. Baker," Ben, the bartender, greeted.

"Hey, Ben," I said, still looking down at my phone.

"You want your usual?" he asked.

"Make it a double," I murmured.

"You got it," Ben replied.

"Rough day?" a soft, familiar voice asked.

I looked up and my eyes were locked with the woman I was just admiring on my phone. It was as if she'd materialized from off of my phone and was now several seats away from me.

"You have no idea," I said, turning my phone off with a chuckle.

"Wedding planning can't be easy," she said.

"Especially when things suddenly start going wrong," I muttered before looking back at her. "So, you've heard about all the wedding buzz going on up here this week?"

There was a look I couldn't quite decipher in her eyes. It almost looked like disappointment. But she blinked and that pretty smile was back on her face as she nodded and said, "I have. Congratulations."

"I'll be sure to pass it on."

"I'm sorry?"

"The congratulations," I said. "I will pass it on to the bride and groom."

"Wait," she said, turning to face me, a look of confusion on her face. "Are you not Mr. Porter?"

"I am," I said with a nod. "But the Mr. Porter getting married this weekend is my brother."

Her mouth dropped open and then she clamped it shut. "I'm sorry. When Sandra mentioned Miss Porter's brother was getting married...and then when Daniel referred to you as Mr. Porter, I just assumed you were one in the same. I wasn't aware there was more than one brother."

"There is. My brother Mason is the one getting married," I said, getting off of my stool and moving to sit in the one right next to her. I held my hand out to her. "I'm Maverick Porter. Very much single."

"Peyton Baker," she said, as she slid her hand into mine. She smiled as we shook hands. "Nice to meet you... again...Maverick Porter Very Much Single."

"Not very subtle there, huh?" I asked sheepishly, as I released her hand.

"No," she said, shaking her head and grinning. "But I like it."

Ben came over and slid a drink in front of Peyton and then passed me my drink. We both thanked him and after he left, Peyton asked, "So, what's going wrong with the wedding? Groom getting cold feet?"

I laughed at her question. "Nah, nothing like that. The groom has *been* ready." I opened my mouth to tell her about what was going on, but then stopped and shook my head. "I don't wanna dump all this shit on you. You're here to enjoy your stay...And maybe find your muse."

"Ahhh, so it was *you* who saw my post and put a heart on it," she said, smiling at me before taking a sip of her drink. I watched as those full, pouty lips wrapped around the edge of the glass as she took a sip and salacious thoughts of what other things those lips might be capable of doing filled my head.

"It was," I said, picking up my own glass and taking a sip to hopefully cool myself off a little bit. "Your man took a great photo."

She threw her head back and laughed. "Again, with the 'subtlety,'" she teased. "No man. Just me, a tripod and a wireless remote. I am also very much single."

"Good to know," I replied and we sat there getting lost

in each other's eyes for a moment. I was the first to break contact. "So, how's the search for your muse going?"

"Uh uh," she said, shaking her head. "I'm not sharing my woes unless you're gonna share yours first. Maybe I can help."

"I appreciate the offer," I said as I stared down into my glass of bourbon. "But unless you know a caterer who can make magic happen in a few days…"

"Actually…" she said slowly, causing me to look up at her and find her staring at me with a smirk on her face.

"Yoooo," I said, turning to face her. Our knees bumped and heat raced up my leg and straight to my dick. But I had to focus on more important matters at the moment. "Are you for real?"

"Well, I can't make any guarantees," Peyton said as she pulled out her phone and pressed on her screen. "But…"

She held up her finger.

"Hey Bee…Yes…I *am* having a good time. Yes…would you…" She rolled her eyes, but still had a smile on her face as she tried her hardest to get a word in. "I need to ask you something important. No, I'm fine…*Bianca!*" she laughed. "Would you listen? Damn! So, I know this is *super* short notice but is Cole available this weekend for a wedding up here at Noir Cove and if not is there another caterer he could recommend. One of the owners is getting married and their caterer flaked on them. Uh huh…huh…yeah, I'll wait." She looked up at me and covered the phone as she said quietly, "She's talking to him now."

I sat there watching, waiting and anticipating a response.

A minute later, Peyton was nodding and holding up a thumbs up sign to me. "Fantastic!" she said into the phone. "I will forward your information to them. Thanks, you guys."

She hung up and I looked at her in disbelief.

"What the hell just happened?" I asked.

"My best friend – who actually gifted me the voucher for my trip here – is married to one of the best chefs I know, and he happens to be a caterer as well. He said he can do it."

"Are you serious?"

"Yep," Peyton said, grinning at me. "Told ya I could help."

I sat there and stared at her for another long moment in shock. Without thinking, I suddenly stood up and pulled Peyton into my arms, wrapping her in a tight bear hug.

She let out a cute laugh as she wrapped her arms around me, returning my hug.

"Thank you," I said, my nose buried in her curls, taking in the sweet honey scent.

"My pleasure," Peyton said against my chest.

I came to my senses and released her.

"Sorry," I said. "I'm just so damn grateful that you made that happen."

"It's fine," Peyton said, clearing her throat as we sat back down. She held her phone up. "Here, let me get your contact info, so I can send you Cole's."

I held up my phone and tapped it against hers and a moment later, her contact card showed up on my screen.

"Got it!" she said. "I'll send his information now."

As she was sending the information, I shot a quick text to my sister.

> I found a caterer.

MONICA

> Are you for real?! So quickly?! How? Who is it?

My phone pinged, alerting me that I'd received the contact information for Peyton's caterer friend. I copied the information and went back to my message with Monica.

> Sending you the info now. Just tell them you're the one who Peyton called about for the Noir Cove wedding.

MONICA

> Peyton? Who's Peyton? Why does that name sound familiar?

> I'll fill you in later, call the caterer.

MONICA

> Okay. I love you. You're the best brother for today.

> Love you too.

I clicked out of the text app and went to my phone app and called the front desk.

"Mr. Porter? How can I help you?"

"Hey Sandra? I need you to set up a deluxe package at the spa for one of our guests."

I watched as Peyton quickly shook her head and tried to reach over to me and grab my arm. I playfully swatted her away.

"Maverick!" she whisper-yelled but I ignored her.

"Of course, Mr. Porter. Which guest?"

"Miss Peyton Baker in the Amani suite."

Peyton sat back, giving up on her attempt to stop me.

"I'll get that in right away," Sandra said.

"Don't charge her," I said. "The package is on us."

"Yes, sir."

"Thanks, Sandra," I said and hung up the phone.

"You *really* didn't have to do that," Peyton said.

"It's the *least* I can do," I said. "You've truly saved the day."

"Every couple deserves to have their wedding go off without a hitch," she replied as she finished her drink and placed her glass down on the bar.

I tipped my head to her empty glass. "Would you like another drink?" I asked.

"That would be nice actually," Peyton said.

"Aye Ben?" I called out. Ben turned to face me, and I said, "Another round for us, please."

"You got it," Ben said.

"And put Miss Baker's drinks on my tab." I turned to face her and noticed her mouth open to protest. "Don't argue," I said.

She clamped her mouth shut and silently acquiesced.

"Now that you've helped solve my problem," I started. "Tell me about this lost muse of yours."

"I'm *definitely* gonna need another drink for that tale," she said.

Right on cue, Ben was back with our second round of drinks.

He gave us a knowing smile before backing away to leave us to our private conversation.

"I saw on your profile that you're a romance author…?"

"Well…these days it feels more like I *used* to be a romance author," she muttered before taking a sip of her drink. "These days…the words just seem…lost. It seems like I've just been dealing with writer's block nonstop."

"I'm sorry," I said, watching the forlorn look on her

face. Even though we'd only just met, I already hated seeing her look so sad.

There was a strong urge inside of me that wanted to do whatever I could to help her.

"Do you have any idea when your block started?" I asked.

Peyton was quiet for quite a while before finally answering. "Probably after my mom passed away last year."

Her words caused an instant ache in my chest. I lifted my glass.

"I know how hard it is to lose a parent."

I could feel her gaze on my face as I took a sip.

"How long has it been?" she asked, quietly.

I cleared my throat. "A few years," I said. "They died within months of each other."

"Oh Maverick. I'm so sorry."

"And I'm sorry for the loss of your mother," I said. "Were you two close?"

"Yeah," she said with a nod. "What about you and your folks?"

"Yeah, we were. What about your dad?"

"Was never in the picture," Peyton said with a shrug of her shoulders. "It was always just me and my mom. I think that's what originally inspired me to write romance. I always wished my mom would find love. Even encouraged it, but...she always insisted that she was fine. She wasn't though. I could always tell that she longed for a companionship that she couldn't get from me. She was an amazing single mom, worked her ass off, supported me and my dreams. But I always wished for more for her, you know?"

"Yeah..." I said contemplatively. "My parents definitely shared a love that seemed like something pulled out of a romance novel. We used to always cringe at how they were all lovey dovey as kids. But as adults we grew to appreciate just how much they still loved on each other."

"They sound like they were amazing," Peyton said.

"They were. I miss them every damn day."

We were quiet for a moment and then Peyton grabbed her glass and tossed the drink back.

"Okay. The time for sadness is over," she declared as she slammed her glass back down on the bar. "Tell me something interesting about yourself."

I smiled at her, more than happy to change the subject.

For the next hour, we sat chatting about everything and nothing.

My sister eventually forced my attention away from our conversation.

"Sorry," I said, checking my phone. "Apparently I'm being summoned for wedding stuff."

"I get it," Peyton said, nodding.

"Thank you again," I said, standing. "For helping us get that whole ordeal straightened out."

"Absolutely," Peyton said, standing as well. "And thanks for keeping me company. I had a great time. Maybe I'll go ahead and cash in on that spa package."

I took her hand in mine and planted a kiss on the back. "If there's anything else we can do to help you find that muse, don't hesitate to ask," I said.

"I'll...keep that in mind," she said, as she gazed up at me with a look of heat in her eyes.

I released her hand and turned to walk away when a thought suddenly hit me.

I turned back to face her as I said, "You know... a boat ride out to the middle of the lake always helps me whenever I need to clear my head. Especially at night when you can gaze up at the stars."

"That sounds...like a great way to find some inspiration. Is there some kind of excursion concierge I need to call to set that up?"

"Leave it up to me," I said, backing away. "That cool with you?"

"Yeah," she said with a nod as she pulled her bottom lip between her teeth. "You've got my number now, so... just text me when and where to meet."

"Bet," I said. "See you soon, Peyton."

"See you soon, Maverick," Peyton replied and then I turned to leave the bar in search for my sister.

Chapter Four

PEYTON

I let out a long groan as the masseuse dug into a hard knot around my shoulder blades.

"Sorry," I said, feeling slightly embarrassed by how I must have sounded.

"Don't be," the masseuse, Casey, said. I could hear the smile in her voice as she continued her amazing ministrations. "Believe me, I've heard worse."

"I bet," I said, sighing as I relaxed my face back into the pillow.

It had been an amazing day at the spa thanks to Maverick. I'd come in and when I'd given them my name, you would have thought I was royalty the way they got to work catering to me.

While I was sure that most of it was just how they generally operated, I also got the feeling that since they knew I'd been sent there pretty much on their boss's dime that they wanted to make sure I was treated with extra special care.

And they definitely went above and beyond.

I'd been given damn near every treatment available and now I was getting the best massage I'd ever experienced.

"Casey…that was so amazing," I said, when we were done. "Your hands are magical."

"Thank you, Miss Baker!" Casey said. "I appreciate the compliment."

She passed me her card.

"Feel free to ask for me personally the next time you come for a visit."

"I absolutely will," I said before turning to head to the locker room area to change back into my clothes.

I'd gotten a manicure, a pedicure, soaked in a mud bath, done a seaweed wrap and finally a hot rock massage and the most amazing facial that had my face looking dewy and glowing.

I changed back into my clothes and headed to a concierge phone to call for a ride back to my tent.

"Peyton!"

I turned to find Monica hurrying over to me.

"Hi, Miss Porter!" I said.

"Please, call me Monica," she insisted. "*Especially* after that huge miracle you pulled off for us and our brother's wedding."

"It was no trouble at all," I said. "I'm glad Cole was available on such short notice."

"Me too!" she said. "And I can't believe *he's* catering. I've been to his restaurant in Ebony Hills and it is spectacular. So anything you need is on us for the duration of your stay."

"I appreciate it but it's truly not necessary," I said, shaking my head. "Maverick getting me a full day at the spa was more than enough."

"You do look ultra-relaxed," Monica said, looking me up and down.

"I am! Casey was my masseuse."

"Ahhh yeah. She's definitely one of our most popular masseuses," Monica said with a nod.

"I see why. I'd definitely make the two hour drive on the regular to get massaged by her."

"Ladies…"

My heart rate instantly sped up at the sound of his voice.

I turned to find Maverick sauntering over to me and Monica.

"Brother dear," Monica said. "We were just talking about Peyton's trip to the spa and how thanks to her hooking us up with Cole for the wedding on such short notice that we'd be covering any other expenses for the rest of her visit."

"And *I*–" I interjected. "Was telling Monica here how that truly is not necessary."

"We won't take no for an answer," Maverick said, his soulful eyes boring into mine, causing a pool of wetness to dampen my panties.

"That's right," Monica said, as Maverick and I continued to just stare at each other. "Well, I've got to go. Tomorrow night is the rehearsal dinner and bachelor and bachelorette parties." She turned to look at Maverick. "You got everything set up?"

"Yes, Wedding Planzilla," Maverick teased, causing me to cough out a laugh. Monica punched Maverick in the arm as she rolled her eyes.

"Whatever," she muttered and turned on her heels. Once she was gone, Maverick turned his gaze back on me.

"So you just got done with the spa?" he asked.

"I did," I said with a nod. I hooked my thumb over my

shoulder. "I was just about to go over to the concierge phone and call for a ride back to my dome.

"I can take you," Maverick offered.

"Are you sure?" I asked. "I wouldn't want to take you away from some other...resort work you need to be attending to."

"Attending to you would be my pleasure," Maverick said, stepping closer to me. "Anything else can wait."

"Umm, sure then..." I stammered, my brain scrambled by his nearness and his scent of sandalwood and something that was distinctly...just him. "I'd love to not have to wait for the shuttle. Thank you."

He placed his hand on the small of my back and guided me outside.

He helped me into the golf cart, just like he'd done on the day I first arrived and then ran around to the other side and got in.

He started the cart and we took off.

"So your day at the spa was good?" Maverick asked.

"It was amazing," I said. "Thank you."

"Don't thank me," Maverick said, a smirk curving up the side of his mouth.

We fell into a comfortable silence for the next couple of minutes and like every other time I took this trip to and from my lodging, I was enchanted by the sight of everything around me.

"It is absolutely stunning out here," I said. "I can't believe you grew up in all of this."

During our chat at the bar the day before, Maverick had told me about the origins of Noir Cove and how his parents had bought the land when he and his siblings were kids. At one point it had been a summer camp for kids, but they'd fallen on hard times and had to shut it down.

Years later, they decided to reopen and rebrand,

gearing it towards adults, and that's how Noir Cove came to be.

"They always liked to say that they were ahead of the 'glamping' game," Maverick told me. "Said they were offering it before 'glamping' was even a word or a trend."

"Sounds like it," I'd replied, captivated by his conversation.

I definitely hadn't wanted our time together to end. Talking with Maverick had been…refreshing and fun.

But admittedly I'd been eager to get back to my tent because…

"I wrote last night," I confessed quietly.

Maverick's head whipped in my direction, a wide smile spreading across his face, revealing his perfect straight white teeth. They were almost blinding against his dark skin.

"Yeah?" he said, seeming genuinely interested.

"Yeah," I said, nodding, tucking my hair that was blowing in the wind behind my ear. "I mean it wasn't much. But…I didn't absolutely hate it enough to delete it all."

"That sounds like progress…?" Maverick said, more in a questioning tone.

"It is," I assured him with a nod.

"Well then congrats, Peyton," Maverick said as he reached over to give my knee a gentle pat.

"Thanks," I replied, hoping the breathlessness I felt didn't come through my voice.

We pulled up to my dome tent and Maverick parked the cart, hopped out and came around to help me get out.

"I'm glad I ran into you," Maverick said as we walked up the steps to my door. "I was going to text you."

"Yeah?" I asked. Why did him telling me that make me want to smile all giddily?

"Yeah. I was going to ask if you were free tonight for that boat ride?"

I shrugged. "Sure. I don't have any set plans for while I'm here. Kinda just tryna go with the flow, ya know?"

"Cool," Maverick replied, smiling at me. "So I'll be back in a few hours to pick you up? Around sunset?"

"You're taking me for the boat ride?" I asked. A part of me had hoped he would.

"Unless you're not comfortable with that?" Maverick asked.

"No!" I said, way too quickly. "I mean…yes…I mean…" I blew out a breath. "I would like that very much. I just didn't want to assume that you would be taking me out on the lake. With you being one of the owners of the resort and your brother's wedding in a couple days, it just seems like your plate is full."

"I will always make time for things that I want to do," Maverick said, stepping closer to me.

Our bodies weren't touching, but the energy radiating back and forth between us was palpable.

I nodded and swallowed. "Well then, I will see you in a few hours," I said, taking a step back.

Maverick nodded and I turned to unlock my door. I hurried into the tent and pressed my back against the door, while I pressed my hand against my chest, feeling my heart racing. I didn't move until I heard his cart drive off.

I found myself smiling as I headed to grab my laptop.

Knowing that I'd be spending the evening out on the lake beneath the stars with Maverick made me even more excited about this little excursion than I'd been before.

Chapter Five

MAVERICK

The next few hours passed by in a blur. I did my best to focus on my tasks of work and helping with the last minute details for Mason and Tatum's wedding, but all I could think about was Peyton and our upcoming time together.

An hour before I was supposed to meet back up with her I called my secretary.

"I need you to put together one of the picnic baskets for our boat excursions," I said.

"Sure thing, boss," she said.

"Thanks," I said before hanging up the phone.

"Since when do you schedule the boat excursions?"

I looked up to find Mason standing in my office doorway.

"You always were a quiet and sneaky bastard," I joked, standing. I went around my desk and pulled him into a hug. "Not much longer til the big day. How you feeling?"

"Ready," Mason said, rubbing his hands together after

we came out of our embrace. "But you know that. You gone answer my question about the boat excursion?"

Mason sat down in a chair and kicked his legs up onto my desk. I shoved them back to the ground and went to sit back in my chair.

When I let several more moments go by without answering him, Mason chuckled.

"What's her name?"

"What?" I asked, looking up from my laptop.

"What is her name?" Mason repeated in a louder and slower tone. "This clearly has something to do with a woman. You taking her out on the sunset boat ride for a date?"

"It's not a date," I quickly replied.

Mason studied me for a moment, his eyebrows knitting together before he said, "But you're *wishing* it was."

My brother's scrutiny annoyed the shit out of me. "It's just…part of a thank you for a favor she helped us out with."

"Oh so it's the chick Monica was telling me about? The one who hooked us up with the new caterer for the wedding?" Mason asked. Once we'd gotten everything fixed, we'd let Mason and Tatum know about the situation. Needless to say, they were grateful that Monica and I had worked to make sure it was all taken care of so they didn't have another thing to worry about.

"Yes," I said to Mason. "Her name is Peyton. She's an author and she came to The Cove looking for inspiration for her next book."

"And I'm sure you're more than willing to help '*inspire*' her in any way possible," he said, wiggling his eyebrows suggestively.

"Can you stop?" I said, laughing. "It's not like that. I

just...I told her the lake was a great place to clear your head and find inspiration."

"Ah...I see," Mason said cryptically as he stood.

"You see what?" I asked.

My brother didn't elaborate on his veiled words. "When you see Peyton later on this evening tell her that both Tatum and I are sincerely thankful for her help. If I get the chance, I'd like to thank her in person."

"I'll send along the message."

"Enjoy your date," Mason said, as he headed for the door.

Before I could argue to his retreating back, my phone rang.

"Yes?" I said, picking up the phone.

"The couple's package for the boat ride excursion that you order is ready, sir," my secretary informed me.

"It's not...Thank you," I said instead of attempting to tell her that it wasn't for a couple. "I'll swing by to pick it up soon."

As I hung up the phone, I tried to ignore the fact that the boat ride beneath the stars was one of the most popular excursions for couples, which is why we went above and beyond to make it a nice, romantic time, and offered these kinds of add-on packages that included finger foods, wine and a blanket, which made for a great opportunity to cuddle up together.

Not that *I* was trying to do any of that, I said to myself. I was just trying to make it an all-around enjoyable experience for Peyton...not *romantic*...

You gone keep tellin' yo self that lie...my brain argued, as I continued thinking about what my brother had said after I'd denied that this whole thing was a date.

But you're wishing it was...

WANDERLUST

Not long after my little chat with my brother, I left work and drove the short distance to my place that was located on the property of Noir Cove but away from all of the resort areas to shower and change. I gave myself one final once over in the mirror, taking in the black cargo shorts and linen button down shirt.

I grabbed my phone and went to find Peyton's name and shot her a text.

> Be there in about twenty minutes.

PEYTON

> Can't wait! See you soon.

I grinned at her text, thinking about how I couldn't wait either.

Once again, my brother's nagging words popped into my head.

As if his annoying ass could sense he was currently invading my thoughts, Mason shot me a text.

MASON

> Will Peyton still be here on Saturday?

> I don't know. Why?

MASON

> Your sister and soon-to-be sister-in-law still keep asking me if you're bringing a plus one.

I groaned at his text. Both Monica and Tatum had been on my case about it too. I'd told them since I was the best man in the wedding there was no real reason for me to really concern myself with bringing a date since I'd be busy with my duties.

But that hadn't stopped them from asking and also trying to set me up, which I'd adamantly refused.

I looked at my phone when I saw Mason had texted again.

MASON

> Just sayin'... if she's still around, maybe ask her to be your plus one. That'll get the ladies off your case and you'll get that date you clearly want.

> You just have a solution for everything, huh?

MASON

> Usually.

I stood there thinking about his suggestion. The truth was I found myself extremely attracted to Peyton. And even though our upcoming outing wasn't technically a date, I found myself doing all of the things that I would do if this were, in fact, actually was. Including ordering that damn couple's package for the boat ride.

Shaking that thought out of my head, I shot a text back to my brother.

> I'll think about it.

I shoved my phone into my pocket and left my bedroom, snatching my keys up as I headed for my garage.

I drove back over to the resort to pick up the picnic

basket for our boat ride before driving to the other side of the lake where the luxury dome tents were.

I pulled up to Peyton's tent, got out and quickly made my way up to the porch and lightly knocked on her door.

A moment later, the door swung open and I was once again greeted by that beautiful smile that had constantly been at the forefront of my mind since we'd met a couple days ago.

She looked amazing in a bright yellow short-sleeved, off-the-shoulder crop top that showed off her midriff as well as a pleasing amount of cleavage. She paired the top with a bright yellow skirt that stopped around her shins and was wearing a pair of white Chuck Taylors. Her curly hair was pulled up into a messy bun at the top of her head, a few tendrils cascading around her face.

"Wow," I said, taking her in from head to toe.

"This isn't too much for the boat ride, is it?" she asked as she twirled around in a circle. I swallowed when I saw her bare skin peeking out from behind the big bow tied at her back.

"No," I said, shaking my head as she turned back to face me, waiting on my response. "You look…like sunshine."

Her smile widened as I palmed my forehead. "That was corny as fuck," I muttered.

"No," Peyton giggled. "It was an amazing compliment. Thank you."

"Are you ready to head out?" I asked.

"Yes," Peyton said with a nod.

We headed for my SUV and I opened the passenger door for her. Once I was in the driver's seat, I headed to the dock, where the boats for rent were located.

I parked the SUV and after we got out, Peyton's

eyebrows raised in intrigue when she saw me pull the picnic basket from out of the back seat.

"Just a few things to nibble on while we're chillin' on the lake," I said.

Her lip quirked up in a sexy little grin. "How thoughtful of you."

We turned and made our way to the dock and were greeted by one of the dock workers.

"Evening, Mr. Porter," he said.

"Hey Jimmy."

Jimmy turned to Peyton.

"Evening, Miss."

"Peyton," she said. "Nice to meet you."

"Likewise," Jimmy said, looking back at me. "We've got your boat all ready."

"Thanks, Jimmy," I said. I placed my hand on Peyton's back _ my hand heating from the contact of her bare skin – and guided her down to the small motorboat waiting at the end of the dock.

"What's up?" I asked when I saw a look on her face that I couldn't quite read. "Is something wrong?"

"No," she laughed. "Nothing at all. I don't know why but in my mind, for some silly reason, I was thinking we'd be going out on the lake in a rowboat."

I threw my head back and laughed. "I mean, we *do* offer those, but...Nah," I said, shaking my head. "This will get us out to the middle of the lake way faster so we can enjoy our time out there for longer. With no strain on these here arms. I've already worked out once today."

Peyton's gaze drifted down to my arms for a moment and then back up to my face, before she nodded her head.

"Can't have you overworking those guns," she teased, as she placed her hand in my outstretched one. I helped her onto the boat and then got on afterward.

Peyton sat down on one of the seats and I placed the basket next to her before heading over to the open-cockpit.

The boat came roaring to life when I started her up, and the jerking of the boat as we took off caught Peyton by surprise. She let out a loud, melodious laugh as we jetted through the water across the lake.

Her laughter died down and a serene smile rested on her face as I continued to drive the boat towards our destination. Those small tendrils of hair hanging down whipped around her face in the wind as she gazed out at the water and mountains off to the west.

The sky was filled with an amalgam of colors – oranges and pinks and purples and blues – and a few stars were already beginning to make their appearance.

I slowed the boat down and shut off the motor, and we were instantly shrouded in silence.

"I never get tired of this sight," I said, coming from around the cockpit to sit down across from Peyton.

"I see why," she sighed as she looked up to the sky. "This is...stunning."

"I spent quite a bit of time out here after my parents passed," I said, as I turned my own gaze up to the sky. "For some reason, I could somehow feel their presence out here stronger than any other place."

I took my eyes off the slow moving clouds in the sky and found Peyton staring at me.

"Sorry," I said. "I hope I'm not tanking the mood."

"You're not," Peyton said, reaching over to place her hand on my thigh. "And don't ever apologize for talking about your parents. I can tell how special they were to you."

"They were," I said. "Thank you."

She gave my thigh a gentle squeeze, and her soft touch caused my dick to stir.

"Would you like a glass of wine?" I asked, shifting so that her hand would ease off of my thigh.

"I would love one," she said. I lifted the top of the wicker basket, and she took it and opened it further and peeked inside. "What else ya got in there?"

"Have a look," I said, as I pulled the wine and two glasses out.

Peyton reached in and grabbed a few canapés and put them on the small plates, while I opened the wine and filled our glasses.

I passed her glass to her, she passed me a plate and we sat in silence for a few minutes, sipping on our wine and nibbling on our food as the bright colors faded away leaving the sky dark and now glittering with stars.

"I don't think I've ever seen so many stars in my life. And the moon!" Peyton gushed as she looked up again. She looked back at me. "Thank you for suggesting this. It's so peaceful and beautiful."

"You're welcome," I said, after I finished eating another hors d'oveuvre . "So. How goes the writing?"

"It's…going," she said.

"Still struggling?" I asked.

"Not nearly as much," she said. "Every writing session seems to get better and longer. The writer's block seems to finally be lifting."

"That's good to hear," I said. I paused for a moment before asking, "Have you ever considered shifting your perspective on what you consider 'writer's block'?"

"How so?" Peyton asked, as she finished off her glass of wine. I offered her a refill and she nodded, holding up her glass.

As I filled her cup I continued. "Well. Have you ever considered that maybe your muse has just been…resting or hibernating?"

"Hmm?" she said, bringing her wine glass to her lips. "'Hibernating'."

"It might feel like she's abandoned you because she's quiet during the times you've thought you needed her the most when you were ready to write. But maybe she's taking the time to just marinate and let all the awesome thoughts in your head get good and seasoned or something…" I shrugged. "I don't know. I'm kinda just rambling here. I've never considered myself creative so take everything that I'm saying with a grain of salt."

"No," Peyton said, shaking her head. "That is actually…an *extremely* creative and, to be perfectly honest, profound way to look at things. And I feel like if I'm able to shift my perspective like you suggested…and take my muse's silence as a time of rest and marinating rather than a time of abandonment, maybe it will be easier to give us both some grace, and actually allow myself to rest and rejuvenate along with her during that time rather than worry when I can't really hear her. It'll be easier said than done and it's gonna take some practice."

"But practice makes progress," I chimed in.

"Practice makes progress," she repeated and then held up her glass. "To progress."

"To progress," I said, clinking my glass against hers.

Peyton wrapped her arms around herself and when I noticed the way she began to slightly shiver, I grabbed the blanket. "Here," I said as I stood and whipped it open.

"You just came fully prepared, huh?" she said, as I wrapped the blanket around her shoulders.

"It gets cold out here at night," I said, rubbing her arms to help warm her up. "Even in the summer time. Maybe we should go ahead and head back to shore."

Even though I'd made the suggestion, I was far from ready for our time together to be over.

"Would you like to go out for dinner after this?" I asked.

"Yes," Peyton said without hesitation. "The food in the basket was tasty, but I'm still starving."

Right on cue, the sound of her stomach growling cut through the silence we'd been shrouded in.

I threw my head back and laughed, the sound echoing across the lake. "Aight, let's get back to shore so we can get you fed."

I went back to the cockpit, restarted the boat, spun the steering wheel and then pushed the throttle to accelerate the boat to get us back to shore, eager to get the next part of our evening together started.

Chapter Six

PEYTON

I bobbed my head to the neo soul lo-fi music streaming through the car stereo as Maverick drove us into downtown Umber Bluffs.

I couldn't stop thinking about how much I was enjoying spending time with him. Even though we hadn't done much during our encounters, each time we were together, I was wanting that time to go on and on.

Which is why I'd happily said yes when he'd asked if I wanted to go out for dinner after our boat ride together.

The boat ride, I thought, sighing wistfully.

"You good?" Maverick asked.

I looked over to find him staring at me as we waited at a red light.

"I'm great," I said, smiling at him.

Maverick's lips curled up into a sexy smile as he turned his focus back on to the road and started driving again when the light turned green.

Meanwhile, my thoughts went back to our time on the boat.

He'd been right about it being a great place to clear my head. I'd honestly discovered that by just sitting on my tent porch that faced the water. I'd woken up this morning, grabbed my laptop and meditated outside, listening to the water as it flowed on the lake.

But there was definitely something that was undeniably magical about being on that boat, with the water surrounding us on all sides, the stars twinkling brightly in the ink black night sky.

I thought back to Maverick's advice on shifting my perspective about my muse. It was truly an eye opening thought.

And to be frank, it had been a huge turn on.

Even now, thinking about it had my pussy pulsing out 'fuck me' in Morse code. I shifted in the plush leather seat, mentally trying to will the throbbing to ease up.

But it had been so damn long since I'd been with a man that now my hormones seemed to be in overdrive ever since I'd met Maverick.

There was no denying it...

I wanted this man.

I had no intentions of hooking up with anyone while on this trip.

But the more time I found myself spending with Maverick, the more my attraction to him grew.

But a part of me was hesitant to act on that attraction.

While I suspected the feeling wasn't one-sided, I also wondered if he was just being polite because I'd helped him and his family out with linking them up with Cole for the wedding.

Another part of me wondered if it was a common

practice of his to take women who were staying at his resort out regularly.

Even though I didn't know him well, he didn't give off that type of vibe.

I was still pondering this as we arrived at the restaurant, went in and were seated by the hostess.

"This place is nice," I said, looking around at the small intimate restaurant.

"Yeah. It's one of my favorite places to come," Maverick said, picking up his menu.

I picked up mine as well as I began to probe, "Bring a lot of ladies that come to the resort here?"

"That's not something I usually do," Maverick said. I peeked over my menu to find him staring at me.

"I'm sorry," I said. "I didn't mean to offend you. I was just…curious on whether or not…" I waved a finger back and forth between us. "…this is a regular practice of yours."

"It's definitely not," he said, with a smirk. "In fact, I try to make it a habit *not* to…interact with guests in…" This time he waved his finger back and forth between us. "…this sort of way. The potential trouble it can lead to is just never worth it."

"Understandable for sure," I said.

We were interrupted by the waiter coming over. We gave him our drink orders and picked out a couple of appetizers and picked up our conversation once he left.

"So then this is all still just a 'thank you' then," I said, looking at my menu again. "For helping you guys out of a jam."

When Maverick didn't respond right away, I looked up to find him staring at me.

"I wish I could say that's all this was," he admitted.

"But…?"

"Don't get me wrong, I'm eternally grateful for what you did. As are my siblings and my future sister-in-law by the way. But if I said this was just my way of thanking you for that, it would be a lie."

"Oh."

"I've enjoyed our time together," Maverick said, reaching across the table to take my hand in his. His thumb gently glided across my knuckles as he continued talking. "And when we're not together, I can't stop thinking about you or thinking up ways to spend more time with you."

"What about your rule of not getting involved with guests?" I asked, my heart pounding with excitement in my chest.

"It seems...you're the exception to that rule."

"I...see..." I said quietly.

"Peyton," Maverick said, as he squeezed my hand.

I looked up to find him staring at me.

"You asked the question, and I answered it honestly," Maverick started. "But...if you're not on the same page as I am in regard to..." He once again waved a finger between the two of us. "...this, I completely understand."

"I've enjoyed spending time together as well," I said. "A lot."

"Yeah?" he asked, smiling at me.

"Yeah. I was glad when you asked me out to dinner. I wasn't ready for our time together to be over."

"Neither was I," Maverick said.

The waiter returned with our drinks and appetizers, and we gave him our food orders.

"So," he said after he'd taken a sip of his bourbon and picked up an appetizer. "I have a confession to make."

"Do tell," I said, lifting my martini to my lips. There was a look of mischief in his eyes.

"I started reading one of your books," he confessed, causing me to choke on my drink.

"Oh shit!" he said, hopping up and coming around to my side of the table as I coughed. "Are you okay, Peyton?"

"I…I'm fine," I assured him. I caught my breath and cleared my throat a few times and then took a sip of water. My body suddenly felt extremely hot as he rubbed my back. "Truly. I'm fine. Your confession just caught me a bit off guard and caused my drink to go down the wrong pipe. I promise I'm okay."

Once he could tell I was truly fine, an amused smirk curved up on those sexy lips of his and he went to sit down.

"So," I said, clearing my throat again and trying not to fan my now extremely flush face. "Uh, which book are you, uh, reading?"

"You are blushing like a motherfucker right now!" he teased.

"Stop it!" I said, throwing my cloth napkin at him as he laughed. "I just…I don't know a lot of men who read my books. This territory is a bit uncharted for me."

"Well…they *should* be reading them." He told me the title of the book he was reading and then added, "You nasty, girl."

"Shut up!" I said, hiding my face behind my hands.

"Aight, lemme stop messin' with you," Maverick chuckled. "Seriously though. You are an amazing writer."

"You really think so?" I asked, looking up at him again.

"Absolutely. I barely got any work done in my office today, cause I was so damn caught up in your book. And those sex scenes…" He shook his head. "Woo."

"Well…thank you," I said. "They can be difficult to write for me."

"Why?" Maverick asked.

I shrugged as I picked at an appetizer. "Sometimes it feels like I'm...a fraud."

"How so?"

I shrugged again. "I write all of these...steamy scenes. Yet, the steam is...nonexistent for me in real life these days."

Maverick didn't respond, he just stared at me, a look on his face I couldn't read.

"And now I'm thoroughly mortified that I just told you that," I mumbled as I finished off my drink and desperately looked around for the waiter, cause I needed a refill immediately.

"Hey," Maverick called out to me. I kept my eyes on the table until he reached across the table and grabbed my hand again as he said, "Peyton. Look at me."

My gaze slid up to his eyes.

"You have *nothing* to be embarrassed about," he said. "And I don't believe you're a fraud. Even though you're writing fiction, there's something about your words that are so damn...real. So raw...so sensual. It's honestly quite fascinating to dive into that beautiful mind of yours through your books." He paused for a moment before adding, "And I'm sure you'll find someone that'll bring that steam back into your life one day real soon."

"You think so?"

"Without a doubt," he said huskily.

Once again, his words had my pussy weeping with desire and ready to ask him if he was willing to be the one up for the challenge.

I was ready for 'one day real soon' to be right fucking now.

This man had me ready to jump over the damn table and climb into his lap and do some incredibly lewd things to him in public.

Instead, I gently slid my hand away from his as I asked, "Do you always have just the right thing to say?"

"Definitely not," he chuckled, taking a sip of his drink. "So where do you get your inspiration to write?"

I used his question as a way to let my overheated body cool the hell down a bit.

"Everywhere to be honest," I said. "Music, other books, people watching?"

"People watching?" Maverick repeated.

"Yeah. It's actually one of my favorite brainstorming exercises to do. I'll just look around and find people to watch and create stories about them in my head. Maybe jot done some notes if it feels like it could actually make for a good story.

"Interesting," Maverick said, contemplatively. He looked around and after a few moments, he tipped his chin to a couple a few tables over. "Those two over there. Tell me their story."

I looked over at the couple and grinned.

"Oh they've definitely gone on a few dates," I said, as we watched them talk. The man slid his hand over and took the woman's hand in his and the woman grinned at him. "It looks to be going *extremely* well."

"How well?" Maverick asked.

My gaze went back to Maverick and I found him staring at me with such an intense gaze that it caused my nipples to instantly harden.

I hesitated before finally answering. "Well enough that she plans on inviting him back to her place for the night."

One of Maverick's eyebrows quirked up in intrigue, a panty-melting smile forming on his lips. "Is that so? And does he accept her invitation?"

"I hope so," I said. "Their chemistry has been building up over several chapters. I don't think they'll be able to resist giving into their attraction for much longer."

"I'd have to agree with you on that," Maverick said.

We continued staring at each other for another tense long moment, before he licked his lips and spoke again.

"Peyton?"

"Yes?"

"Would I be wrong in assuming that we're no longer just talking about that couple over there?" he asked.

"No," I admitted. "You wouldn't be wrong."

Maverick nodded. "That's good to know. Because from the moment we've met, I've found myself extremely attracted to you. I haven't been able to get you out of my mind. Some of the thoughts I've had of you…"

When he just let that sentence trail off, I asked him, "What kind of thoughts?"

He looked up at me, his eyes full of lustful desire. "If I told you, they might scare you."

"I don't scare easily," I boldly retorted.

A devilish grin spread across his lips, as he said, "I'd much rather show you. It would be much more fun that way."

"I see," I said, as the throb between my legs intensified. "Well then maybe we should—"

The sound of the waiter's voice damn near made me jump out of my skin.

I'd been so lost in my conversation with Maverick and how it had taken this seductive turn that everything around us seemed to have faded away.

The waiter placed our food on the table as he repeated our orders back to us. I barely heard a word he was saying and my appetite for food had been replaced by a different kind of hunger.

"Does everything look good?"

"Yes," Maverick said slowly, still looking at me. "Yes, it does."

I knew he wasn't talking about the food. The look in his eyes made it clear that the only thing he was wanting to devour at the moment was me.

And I was more than eager to feed him.

"Is there anything else I can get you?" the waiter asked.

We stared at each other for another long, sensual moment. Maverick nodded his head and I knew we'd just come to a silent agreement. I plastered a smile on my face and looked up at the waiter. "Some to-go boxes. Please."

The waiter looked surprised by my request.

"Oh. Sure," he stammered as he looked back at the food he'd just placed on the table. "Uh, is everything okay?"

"Everything is fine," I assured him. "Something just came up."

I looked back at Maverick and saw the amused smirk on his face as he discreetly shifted in his seat.

My gaze dropped down to the table, which was covering Maverick's lap, preventing me from getting a glimpse at that particular 'something' that had come up. I was eager to get him back to my tent to see it with my own eyes.

"Can I interest you in a dessert to go?" the waiter asked.

"No," Maverick said, a gruffness in his tone that made my skin tingle. "Just the check please."

"Of course," the waiter said, nodding his head as he picked the plates back up. "Let me hurry and get these boxed up and get the check for you guys so you can be on your way."

"Thank you," we both said, before he retreated to get the things we'd asked for.

After the waiter left, I stood. "I'm going to run to the restroom before we head out," I said.

Maverick nodded, his eyes boring into me.

I turned and hurried to the restroom.

After I relieved myself, I washed my hands, and stared at myself in the mirror.

I reapplied my lipstick and ran my hands down my skirt.

"Girl, you look amazing!" a woman said as she came out of the stall and over to the sink to wash her hands.

I realized it was the woman from the couple I'd created the story about.

She was even prettier up close and I returned her compliment. "You look great too."

"And your date!" she added. "Yum!"

Yum was definitely an appropriate word, because Maverick Porter had my damn mouth watering.

"Have a great night," I said before leaving the restroom.

When I came out, Maverick was standing there, a bag in his hand.

"Oh!" I said, pressing my hand to my chest.

"Thought you said you didn't scare easily," he teased.

"Ha ha," I said. "I just didn't expect to see you right here."

"It's by the exit," he explained. "And I already settled the check."

"Eager to get out of here, huh?" I said.

"You have no idea," he said roughly. "You ready?"

"Yes."

He slid his free hand around mine and led the way outside.

"Have a great night!" the hostess called to our backs as we left the restaurant.

There was a headiness that hovered between us as we walked to his SUV.

We got to my side of the car and a gasp slipped from my lips when Maverick suddenly spun me around and pressed me against the car door as he dropped his mouth down onto mine in a mind-numbing kiss.

I immediately returned the kiss, wrapping my arms around his neck as his free hand snaked around my waist and pulled me against his body.

I could feel his erection pressing into my belly, and I pushed my body against him even more.

His tongue slid into my mouth, swirling around my own tongue. I let out a whimper as he bit down on my lip and slowly began to ease his mouth away.

He pressed his forehead against mine as we both sucked in deep breaths of air.

"I'm sorry," he said. "But I couldn't wait another minute to kiss you. You are just…so fucking irresistible."

"The feeling is mutual, so don't apologize," I said, sliding my hands down to his chest. I could feel his heart pounding beneath my fingertips. "That was…even better than I've imagined."

"So you've imagined kissing me?" he asked, pressing his lips against my neck.

"I've imagined doing a lot of things to you," I whispered.

Maverick pulled away from me and looked down at me.

"Like what?" he rumbled.

I let a seductive smile curl on my lips as I repeated his own words back to him. "I'd much rather show you. It would be much more fun that way."

I shivered when he let out a low growl before he hit the key fob and opened my door.

I climbed in while he placed the food in the backseat and went around to the driver's side.

He started the SUV and after he began to drive, he reached over and took my hand in his.

The drive back to Noir Cove seemed to take forever and fly by at the same time and soon we were pulling up to my dome. I reached into my purse and pulled out my key card as Maverick got out and came around to open my door for me.

My hands trembled with anticipation as we climbed up the porch steps and I quickly unlocked the door and we went inside.

I turned to face him and before I could get a word out, Maverick palmed my face between his big, rough hands and plied my mouth with another drugging kiss.

I let my purse fall to the floor, freeing my hands to roam his chiseled body. My hands glided up his strong forearms before moving up to squeeze his biceps. They finally landed on his broad shoulders, and I held onto them as I rocked my body against his.

"Tell me what you want, Peyton?" Maverick muttered against my lips.

My hand slid down between our bodies and I wrapped it around his hard dick that was pressing through his pants.

"This," I said, squeezing it. "I want this."

Maverick crushed his lips against mine again, his tongue gliding along the seam of my mouth and I eagerly opened and took his tongue into my mouth.

My body trembled when I felt his hand caress the bare skin of my back before he tugged and undid the bow that was tied at the back of my top. He pulled my top off and tossed it to the floor and then he eased my skirt off.

Suddenly Maverick picked me up and carried me across the room to the bed where he sat me down. My breathing grew heavy as I watched him kneel down in front of me and take off my shoes and socks.

He placed a kiss on one ankle and then the other ankle. He moved up my body and kissed both of my shins and then both of my knees. He hooked his hands around the backs of my knees and opened my legs wide and I watched as his eyes dilated and he licked his lips.

"Fuck," he groaned. "You smell so fucking sweet, baby."

My head fell back as he pressed a kiss to my right inner thigh and then my left inner thigh.

And then he pressed his nose against my panty-covered pussy and inhaled deeply.

"I need to taste you," he damn near growled. "Peyton."

I lifted my head and looked down to find Maverick gazing up at me from between my thighs.

"May I taste you?"

"Yes," I breathed. "Hell yes."

His fingers hooked into the waistband of my panties, and he began to ease them down. I lifted my hips to help him get them off and when they were gone, he pushed my legs even wider and draped them over his shoulders.

"You're so fucking wet," he muttered. I trembled when he ran a finger down my slick folds and then slid it inside of me. "Is this all for me, baby?"

"Yes," I moaned, rolling my hips as he continued to finger me. "Yesssss."

He spread my lips and dragged the flat part of his tongue against my pussy, slowly licking me.

He groaned and the sound vibrated against my body, sending me into a frenzy.

"Shit...Mav..." I moaned again, grabbing the back of his head. He dipped his tongue in and out of me a few times and then licked me again.

I mewled when he sucked my pearl between his lips.

I gripped the sheets and squeezed my eyes shut as the sensations of pleasure washed over me. My eyes slid open, and my gaze went to the clear ceiling of the dome. I was seeing the literal stars and moon in the sky as I rocked against Maverick's face. He had me seeing stars in the metaphorical sense as he licked, sucked and fucked my pussy into an out of this world orgasm with his mouth.

"Maverick!" I cried out as my body exploded, sending me into an abyss of pleasure.

"That's it," he said, pulling away briefly. "Cum on my tongue, baby."

And then he dove back in, ravishing me, grunting and groaning as I came so hard that my body was shaking uncontrollably.

I tried to push him away, but he locked his big, strong arms around my thighs and held me in place.

"Uh-uh. Don't you fucking run from it," he growled before pulling my clit back between his lips and sucking hard on it causing me to scream his name.

"*Maverick!*"

He didn't ease up until my body collapsed against the bed.

I felt the bed shift as he got up. I slid my eyes open to find him standing over me as he pulled a condom out of his wallet. He tossed it onto the bed and then began to undress.

My mouth watered with each new exposed part of his muscular body being revealed.

When he was finally down to nothing but his boxers, I grabbed the condom and ripped it open just as he removed his last garment of clothing, his dick bobbing deliciously in my line of sight.

I sat up in the bed on my knees and held up the

condom. Maverick nodded and I scooted to the edge of the bed and took his manhood in my hands and slowly rolled the condom onto it.

Maverick let out a low groan when I didn't remove my hand but instead wrapped it tighter around his dick and began to stroke him from the base to the tip. I wanted to taste him, but before I could lower my head, Maverick pulled my hand off of him and climbed back into the bed, laying me on my back.

"I'm gonna cum way too quickly if you keep touching me like that," he said, pressing a kiss to my neck.

I felt the tip of his dick probing at my entrance so I spread my legs wider, inviting him to fill me up.

Maverick's dick slowly eased inside of me, stretching my walls to accommodate him.

"Fuck," he moaned as he slid deeper inside of me. "You're so wet and so tight."

He slowly pulled out until just the tip was inside and then dove even deeper. He continued moving in and out of me at an unhurried pace.

Every cell in my body was on fire as Maverick continued stroking me. His mouth was all over me…his hands were all over me…it was all sending my body into a fabulous frenzy.

"Maverick!" I wailed as I felt another orgasm on the horizon.

"Shit," Maverick groaned as his movements grew wild and out of control. He sat up, tightly gripping my hips as he began to vigorously pound my pussy.

The sounds of our bodies colliding together over and over filled the space and I was sure the guests on the other side of the damn lake could hear my screams of ecstasy.

But I didn't give a damn.

"Peyton!" Maverick muttered as he slammed into me, hitting a spot that had me coming unglued.

Maverick's entire body grew taut and then it relaxed and he eased his body back on top of mine as we both laid there trying to catch our breath. After another minute, he rolled off to the other side of the bed.

I was spent. But in the best way possible.

It had been way too long since I'd been with a man.

But Maverick had definitely made up for lost time for me, I thought as I drifted off to sleep with a satisfied smile on my face.

Chapter Seven

MAVERICK

"No!" Peyton said, throwing her head back and laughing as I showed her the awful school picture. She took my phone and stared at it, still giggling. She looked up at me her eyes filled with mirth. "You were still so cute though."

It was nearly midnight and we were sitting up in bed in the plush complimentary robes, feasting on our food from the restaurant. I'd gone and grabbed it out of the car after Peyton had woken me up for another round of lovemaking, leaving us famished.

We'd been sitting around chatting, chilling and chowin' down on our food that Peyton had reheated in the small microwave in the dome.

We were talking about embarrassing childhood memories, and I told her about the worst picture day I'd ever had thanks to a terrible haircut my mother had given me while she'd been suffering with a cold.

"My siblings still tease me about this shit to this day," I

said, taking my phone back from her. My fingers brushed against Peyton's in the process and the instant spark I felt zinged up through my arm.

Thinking about her soft fingers took me back to earlier in the night when those same soft fingers were wrapped around my dick, stroking me into a frenzied state.

"I can see why," Peyton said, bringing me back to the present. I looked up to find her stuffing her face full of food. Even doing that, she still looked so pretty.

Her lip quirked up and over a mouth full of food she said, "Why are you looking at me like that?"

"I'm sorry I can't help it," I said, shaking my head. "You're so damn pretty."

She rolled her eyes as she chewed her food and swallowed. "Oh, I'm sure," she said in a sarcastic tone. "As I'm shoving food in my mouth like a heathen and this bird's nest on my head."

Her curls were a wild tangled mess now.

"It's gonna take forever for me to wash and detangle my hair. Thanks by the way," she added.

"I'm sorry," I said genuinely. "But it just...smelled so good and felt so good in my hands. Which you didn't seem to complain about when I had a handful of it as I hit it from the back not too long ago."

"Touché," Peyton said with a smirk.

"Still, I really am sorry for messing it up. You need help with it?"

"Are you for real?" she asked.

"Sure. I used to watch my mom detangle my sister's tender-headed ass hair all the time growing up," I said, shrugging. "Unless that's...too weird or too soon or something."

"I think you're just trying to find an excuse to get some in the shower," Peyton teased.

"I hadn't thought about that," I admitted honestly. "But now that you've planted that seed in my head."

Peyton threw her head back and laughed loudly.

"Thank you for the offer," she said. "I'll keep it in mind."

"The help with the hair or the sex in the shower?" I asked. "There's plenty of room for two in there."

She laughed again but sobered up a little bit to answer me. "Both."

I nodded and we fell into a pleasant silence as we went back to eating.

"So," I said finally after I'd been mulling it over since the night before when my brother had texted me the suggestion. "My brother's wedding is tomorrow."

"Oh yeah!" she said, grinning. "Are you excited for your brother?"

"I am," I said. "He loves Tatum so much and can't wait to marry her. It's gonna be an amazing wedding. In part, thanks to you with hooking us up with Cole to cater at the very last minute."

She waved off my words of gratitude. "Stop thanking me," she said.

"One more thank you," I said. "But not from me. Mason and Tatum wanted me to send you their thanks."

"I told you it was my pleasure. No one should have their wedding day ruined...for any reason."

"I can agree with you there."

"I love weddings," Peyton said wistfully. "Watching two people join their lives together...pledging their love together for all eternity."

She looked up at me and blushed. "Sorry for rambling on about weddings."

"Don't apologize," I said. "You kinda made what I want to ask you a bit easier."

"What did you want to ask me?"

"How would you feel about crashing the wedding?"

"Say what now?"

"I'd like you to come to the wedding," I said. "As my date."

"You would?" she asked.

"Yes, I would."

She pulled her bottom lip between her teeth, a look of contemplation on her face.

"Hey, it's totally fine if you're trying to find a way to turn me down. We only just met and if the idea of one of our first dates being a wedding is weird or something—"

"It's not that," Peyton said, cutting me off. "It's just that I was supposed to be checking out tomorrow and heading back to Ebony Hills. I'd love to go with you actually. But staying for the wedding means I'd have to probably stay for another night because I don't care to drive the couple hours back home so late at night."

"Ah," I said nodding. "The tent is already booked for someone else to check into after you."

"I figured as much," Peyton said with a nod.

"You can stay with me," I blurted out.

"What?!" she squeaked.

"Spend the rest of the weekend with me," I said, I moved the now empty cartons of food off to the side and crawled my way over to Peyton. Climbing on top of her, I started to kiss her neck. "I've enjoyed this time I've gotten to spend with you, Pey."

"Same," she breathed as my lips moved to her collarbone. She lifted her hips, pressing her warm pussy against my thigh that was resting between my legs.

"And I'm not ready for our time together to be over," I admitted.

"Neither am I," she confessed.

"Well then," I said, pushing open her robe to reveal her beautiful naked body. "Be my date to the wedding and then come back with me to my place and stay with me for the rest of the weekend."

"Mav," she sighed, as I dropped my head between her breasts. I kissed my way over to one and pulled her hard nipple into my mouth and began to suckle it hungrily.

"How am I supposed to say no when you're doing things like this to me?" she mewled.

"You're not," I growled, as I slid my finger along her slit before pushing it inside of her wetness. "Just say yes."

"Yessss," she moaned loudly.

"Are you saying yes to being my date and spending the weekend with me?" I asked as I continued pumping into her. "Or are you saying yes to what I'm doing to you right now?"

"Both…"

PEYTON

I let out an exhale and paused, leaning down to rest my hands on my knees and catch my breath.

What the fuck made me think this was a good idea?! I asked myself as I stood back up to my full height and glared at the long trail that was in front of me.

Maverick Porter, apparently.

Last night and the early morning hours with him had been amazing. Unfortunately he had to leave me because it was the day before his brother's wedding and as the best man, he had a lot of business to take care of including the wedding rehearsal, rehearsal dinner and bachelor party.

He told me they were driving to Ebony Hills for the

night to party and would be heading back early in the morning.

I'd be lying if I said I wasn't disappointed when I found that information out. With our time together soon coming to an end, I wanted to spend as much time with Maverick as I could.

During our late night chat, Maverick had asked me about all of the things I'd done around Noir Cove when I hadn't been spending time with him and I'd filled him in. I honestly hadn't done too much, but I didn't need to. Just being out here, surrounded by the beautiful nature that Noir Cove was on was enough to refresh, rejuvenate and inspire me to write.

Maverick had also helped inspire me.

Somehow I'd foolishly let that motherfucker inspire me into checking out one of the hiking trails.

I was *not* a hiker.

"Clearly I need to up my cardio," I huffed to myself, as I started walking again.

I lied to myself and said when I got home from my mini retreat that I was going to go online and find one of those treadmills that all the social media girlies used beneath their desks that could raise to standing height.

Pulling out my phone I sat down on one of the benches and shot a text to Maverick.

> I can't believe I let you talk me into a fucking hike.

I hit send and instantly saw the typing bubbles begin to pulse.

MAV

> You good, beautiful?

> No, I'm not good, Maverick. I thought my ass was in shape, but this hike is proving otherwise.

MAV:

> LMAO. I can tell you from personal experience that you've got stamina for days, woman. 😏

> 😳 I think you stole all my stamina. Cause I'm exhausted.

Mav

> How far into the hike are you?

I texted him my location and he texted me back.

MAV

> You're almost there, gorgeous. Keep going. I promise it's worth the hike.

He'd suggested this particular hike because of what I'd find at the end of it. When I asked him what that was, he said it was better if I discovered it myself.

> Next time, you're coming with me. That way you can carry me back to the tent.

Mav

> It's a date. 😉

I stood and took another breath and continued my hike. A few minutes later, I let out a gasp as I stared at a beautiful waterfall in front of me. I lifted my phone, snapped a selfie with the waterfall behind me, and sent it to Maverick.

> This is amazing! 😊

MAV

> I told you it was worth the hike. 😉

I gnawed on my lip nervously going back and forth on whether or not I wanted to text him what I was thinking. Eventually I shook off the nerves and texted him.

> I wish you were here with me.

Staring at the waterfall gave me flashbacks to earlier this morning before we parted ways.

I'd gone to take a shower and to wash my hair and Maverick joined me in the shower. My scalp began to tingle at the memory of Maverick tenderly massaging the shampoo into my scalp. As we stood beneath the shower, my back facing him, he'd taken his time to finger-detangle my long strands of coily hair.

When I'd asked him if he was going to be late for his wedding duties, he'd simply kissed my wet shoulder and said, "I've got time…" before continuing to gently work his fingers through my hair. After rinsing out the shampoo, his hands began to roam my body, cupping and squeezing my breasts in his big strong hands.

Soon he had me bent over in the shower, screaming his name over and over again.

My phone pinging brought me back to the present.

MAV

> I wish I was there with you too, baby.

Seeing 'baby' at the end made a ridiculous ass grin spread across my lips.

Although we'd only known each other for a few short days, the connection between us was strong and undeniable. Hell, I already found myself looking at Noir Cove's website for available dates to make another reservation so I could come back.

And I wasn't wanting to come back just for the scenery.

I hadn't even left yet, and I was already ready to come back to see Maverick again.

It felt crazy, but it also felt good.

I'd written about some of my characters falling fast for one another, but in all honesty that was one of the things that I just considered fiction.

But…was it *truly* possible to fall for someone so damn quickly?

After meeting Maverick, my perspective on that was beginning to shift.

I pulled my backpack off of my back, opened it up and pulled out the blanket that Maverick insisted I take with me. After I spread out the blanket on the grass, I sat down on it and pulled my laptop out of my backpack.

I spent the next hour typing away with the sound of the waterfall as my background music.

Chapter Eight

PEYTON

The sound of my phone ringing stirred me awake. Rolling over, I noticed the time and saw that it was after ten at night. After my writing session at the waterfall, I'd hiked back to my tent, got cleaned up and went into town to find a dress to wear to the wedding since I hadn't packed any formalwear. Thankfully I found a dress quickly because after that hike every muscle in my body was sore as hell.

When I got back to Noir Cove, I ordered room service for dinner. After eating and enjoying a couple glasses of wine, I decided to take a long hot soak in the tub to soothe my aching muscles.

Feeling bold from the wine, I decided to send Maverick a few pictures of how I was spending my evening without him. One was a full body pic of me, strategically covered in bubbles. The next was a pic of just my legs in the shot and my hand holding my glass of wine. The last pic of me was from behind. The camera had focused in on my wine glass on the edge of the tub so I was blurred out in the background but even still the picture was hot as fuck if I do say so myself.

When I sent him the pictures, I used the invisible ink feature and added a text message along with it.

> For your eyes only. 😉 Wish you were here.

Since I knew he was busy with wedding stuff, I didn't expect him to respond right away, so I'd eventually settled in for the evening. I'd started reading a book and must have dozed off.

"Hello?" I said groggily.

"Oh shit, you were sleeping," Maverick's velvety smooth voice said, his handsome face filling my phone screen, waking me and my body up instantly. "My bad."

"No it's fine," I insisted as I sat up in the bed. "Hi."

"Hi," he said, smiling at me.

"Is that Peyton?" I heard in the background followed by Maverick looking over his shoulder, laughing and saying, "Yo…chill…"

"Tell Peyton she's my superhero!" someone shouted.

"Is that your brother?" I asked.

"Yeah, that's his drunk ass," Maverick chuckled. "We just made it to the hotel."

"Ah."

All of sudden there was another face on the screen. He looked a lot like Maverick and I knew it was Mason who was pressing his cheek against Maverick's as he stared into the phone.

"Miss Peeeyyyyttoooon!" he slurred, causing me to giggle. "Nice to finally meet you in person. Well…sorta."

"Nice to meet you too," I said.

"Maverick told me he asked you to be his date to the

wedding," he said. "You know *I* was the one who told him to ask you."

"Oh were you now?" I asked, raising an eyebrow. "Well I appreciate the invite."

Maverick pressed his hand against Mason's face and shoved his brother away.

He turned his attention back to me. "Aye, baby, lemme get this fool settled in for the night and I'll call you when I get to my room."

Before I could respond I heard Mason goading Maverick. "'Baby'? You calling her baby already? Maverick is in loooooove!"

"Shut up, Mase," Maverick said laughing.

Mason started singing a combination of T-Pain's *I'm Sprung* and "Maverick and Pey Pey sittin' in a tree…k-i-s-s…"

Maverick hung up the phone as I continued laughing so hard tears were streaming down my cheeks.

I finally caught my breath and wiped the tears from my face and then sat up in the bed as I eagerly waited for Maverick to call me back.

Thankfully I didn't have to wait for too long.

I answered as soon as the phone rang.

"Hey," I said, hoping I didn't sound too damn breathless.

"Hey, yourself," Maverick replied. I could tell from the slightly glassy look in his eyes that he was tipsy as well, but he clearly hadn't turned up as much as the groom had.

"You have a good time tonight?" I asked.

"I did," he said, nodding his head. "How did your writing by the waterfall go?"

"It went well," I said, smiling. "Although by the time I got back my muscles were screaming."

"That sucks," Maverick said. "If I were there, I'd give you a massage."

"Any excuse to get me naked," I teased.

"Hell yeah!" he said. "Especially after I thought I was gone meet my maker for a minute, thanks to you."

"Thanks to *me*?!"

"Yes," Maverick said. "Thanks to *you*…and those pictures you sent."

My eyes bulged and my mouth formed a perfect O as I gasped.

"Oh my god what?!" I said, alarmed. "What the hell happened?"

"Well," he said, a smirk on his face. "I was at the rehearsal dinner, and I finally got the chance to slow down and check my phone. I noticed that I had several text photos that were hidden with the invisible ink feature, so I tucked the phone in my lap under the table and swiped my finger over the first picture. Just as I was taking in a mouth full of pasta."

"Noooo!" I gasped.

"Yep!" he said, nodding. "Caught me so off guard that I started choking."

I covered my mouth. "Mav!"

"Folks came rushing over to check on me and I had to keep my phone hidden. Then I had to stay seated so I could keep my dick hidden. Cause yeah…couldn't let grandma see what you'd sent and how my body had responded to it."

"Oh my gawd!" I laughed. "I'm sorry. I shouldn't be laughing but…"

I fell onto my side on the bed as I continued laughing.

"Yeah laugh it up," Maverick said in a deadpan tone, but his lips were curved up in a grin.

"Seriously though," I said finally. "I'm glad you were okay."

"Oh I was *not* okay," he said. "Had me ready to drive all the way back there and tear your fine ass up after I got a chance to look at all those pictures."

I pulled my lip between my teeth and smiled coyly at him. "Sorry."

"No you're not," he said. "Had my shit hard as a rock for damn near the rest of dinner. Hell, my shit is brickin' back up right now just thinking about those pics."

My heart started pounding at the same time as my pussy.

"Yeah?" I breathed.

"Hell yeah."

I saw the lust in his eyes and I stared at him through the phone and licked my lips.

"Lemme see."

Maverick's eyebrows shot up. "What?"

"Let me see it," I said, my breathing growing shallow. "I want to see what my pictures did to you."

He stared at me through the screen for another moment and then said, "Hold on."

I watched the screen and listened as he moved around a bit. After a couple of minutes, he had the phone set up to where I could see all of him.

I bit back a moan as I watch him wrap his hand around his long, hard dick.

"Is this what you wanted to see, baby?" Maverick grunted as he began to stroke it from the base to the tip. I watched as he ran his thumb over the tip, spreading a bit of pre-cum over it.

"Yes," I whispered, my hand sliding beneath the covers. I ran my fingers along my clit and a moan slipped out.

"Are you touching yourself, Peyton?" Maverick asked.

"Yes."

"I'm showing you mine," he pointed out. "Now show me yours."

I shoved the duvet blanket down to the foot of the bed and propped my phone up against the blanket. I sat back against the headboard and spread my legs.

"Spread them wider for me, baby," Maverick ordered as he continued stroking his dick. "I want to see every inch of that pretty pussy."

I did as I was told and opened my legs wider as I sank my fingers into my pussy and then massaged my clit with my juices.

"Gotdamn you're so wet," Maverick grunted. "I can see it glistening through the phone. I can hear it too. Shit. Those pictures you sent me were so sexy. Had me wishing I was there with you in that tub, riding my dick."

"Maverick," I whimpered as I slid my fingers deeper inside of me. My eyes fluttered closed and my head fell back against the headboard. "I wish this was your dick inside of me."

"I wish it was too, baby," he said. "I'd bury my face in between your thighs and fuck your pussy with my mouth until you came on my tongue and then I'd bury my dick so fucking deep inside of you."

His words made me even wetter and I started pumping my fingers in and out of me faster and faster. I pressed the heel of my hand hard against my clit.

"Open your eyes, baby," Maverick said. "You said you wanted to see it. Look at it. Look at what you do to me."

I opened my eyes and saw that his movements had sped up just like mine had. Somehow his dick had grown even longer and harder in his hands.

"I can't wait to feel you inside of me again," I said.

"I can't wait either," Maverick rasped. "I love the way your walls feel milking my dick."

"Maverick!" I mewled. "I'm so close."

My breathing was erratic as I stroked myself into an orgasm that had my hips lifting off the bed.

"Fuck, you're so gorgeous when you cum. I wish I was there so I could feel you creaming all over this dick. Peyton!"

Maverick let out a groan and I watched as his seed spilled out of him.

We laid there for several moments, our heavy panting the only sound in the air. I watched Maverick through heavy lids as he grabbed a towel and cleaned himself up.

"That was...fun," I said, sleepily.

"Not as fun as being with you," Maverick said. "But I'll take it."

I covered my mouth as I let out a loud yawn.

"I'll let you go so you can get some sleep," Maverick said.

Even though I was exhausted, I wasn't ready to get off the phone with him. But I knew tomorrow was going to be a long day for him so I simply nodded and said, "Okay."

"When I get back into town in the morning, I will swing by and pick you up so we can take your things over to my place," he said. "I live on the property."

"You do?" I said. "That's so cool."

"Yeah," he chuckled. "I'll see you in the morning, Peyton."

"See you in the morning, Maverick. Goodnight."

"Goodnight, gorgeous. Sleep well and dream of me."

Chapter Nine

PEYTON

I followed Maverick in my car through the wooded area past the main area of Noir Cove and drove for several more miles until we reached a gate that had a 'restricted area' sign posted up on it. Maverick stopped his SUV, rolled down the window and pushed in a code and the gate slowly slid open.

He drove through the gate and then I did so as well, and we continued down a long winding road for another couple of miles before breaking through a clearing. I let out a gasp when I saw the large house in front of us.

"This is amazing," I exclaimed to myself.

His home was a two-story cabin-style home with wrap-around porches on both floors.

Off to the left side of the house was a huge pond. You could see the mountains in the distance.

We continued driving up to the house and Maverick pulled into the garage. I drove into the garage as well, parking in the empty spot next to his SUV. I turned the car off as Maverick got out of his SUV and came around to open my door. As I got out, he grabbed my bags out of the back.

He took my hand in his and led the way through the large garage to the door that took us inside of his massive home.

"Welcome to my place," he said. "Make yourself at home to whatever you'd like."

"Wow," I whispered, looking around at the house.

It was a huge open-floor plan, but even though the space was large, it still felt cozy with the big comfy looking sectional sofa that faced a fireplace in the living room. There was a long dining room table that separated the living room from the kitchen area.

The kitchen was amazing with its long island, double oven and huge stove.

But what really took my breath away was the windows. There were floor to ceiling windows all around, giving us views of the pond and the mountains.

There wasn't a bad view at all, I thought to myself as I went to stare out of one of the windows.

"I had that pond put in when I bought the place," Maverick explained. He pointed at the mountains. "Those mountains belong to the Hamiltons. They own Hamilton Ridge, another resort in Umber Bluffs."

"Oh wow," I said, looking at the mountain again. "Are they like the town rival or something?"

Maverick shook his head. "Quite the opposite actually. We've been friends with them for decades. Our parents were friends with each other, and all of the Porter and Hamilton kids grew up together playing on each other's properties. Summers here on the lake, winters there in the mountains. We're still great friends to this day."

"That's great. And it's great that you both run resorts and aren't competing."

"There's no need. There's room for everyone and we usually cater to slightly different customers. Our customers are here for more of the camping and glamping experience while Hamilton Ridge is a ski resort, so their customers are more into hitting the slopes. And we also offer day passes on a lot of amenities at both resorts, so if there's something we don't have here that they've got at Hamilton Ridge we always refer them over there and they do the same for us."

"So, you actually work together!" I said.

"Yeah, we do," Maverick said with a nod.

"I love that!"

"Come on," Maverick said as he squeezed my hand. "Let me show you the rest of the house."

He led me down to the basement, which was fully furnished. There was a theater room down there as well as a mini bowling alley.

We went back upstairs, and he showed me the rest of the first floor, which included his office that he offered to me to use to write in while I was staying there. Finally, we went up to the second floor. After showing me several different rooms, our last stop was the primary suite.

"This is my room," Maverick said, stepping to the side to let me enter first. The space was masculine, with black and taupe colors all around. But at the same time, it felt warm and inviting.

My eyes went wide when I noticed the massive skylight in the ceiling over the even more massive sized bed that was the centerpiece of the room.

"It's an Alaska King size bed," Maverick said over my shoulder, answering my unasked question as he sat my bags down.

"I didn't even realize there was a bed this damn big," I said. "There's so much room for…activities."

"I guess we'll find out soon enough," Maverick said, wrapping his arms around my waist. He buried his nose into my neck as he confessed, "You're the first woman I've brought back here."

I turned in his arms and looked up into his eyes. "Are you serious?"

"Dead ass. I consider my home a sacred space."

I could see why. Maverick's home was like something out of a magazine or something.

His words made me curious though. "How did *I* earn the honor of being the first to be invited into your sacred space?" I asked, quietly. "We've only known each other for a few days."

"And yet," Maverick said, looking into my eyes with a soul stirring gaze as he pushed a strand of hair out of my face. "It feels like we've known each other for a lifetime."

"Mav," I whispered, his words making my heart skip a beat. I slid my hands up his chest as Maverick's hand gently cupped my cheek, his thumb caressing my bottom lip. He lifted my face and replaced his thumb with his lips, plying my mouth with tender kisses.

I wrapped my arms around his neck and pushed my body closer, feeling his manhood come to life.

And then I felt his phone vibrate in his pocket. He put just enough space between us to grab his phone and mute it.

"Shouldn't you answer that?" I asked, as he continued kissing me.

"It can wait," Maverick muttered as he pulled my earlobe in between his teeth. He'd quickly learned that was a spot that drove me wild. In fact, he'd quickly learned about damn near every erogenous spot on my body that drove me wild.

The phone started ringing again, and I pressed my hands to his chest to gently push him away.

"Mav," I said, looking at him knowingly. "You're the best man."

He blew out a breath and nodded. He gave me one last quick peck on the lips and answered his phone.

"Yes, Monica?"

"Where are you?" I heard her ask through the phone even though she wasn't on speaker.

"I had to handle some stuff," he said, looking at me and I could tell from the look in his eyes that he hadn't handled everything he'd wanted to.

"What stuff?" his sister asked.

"Don't worry about all that," he snapped back.

"Don't you yell at me," she argued.

"I had to make sure Peyton was good," he said finally.

"Oh. Well, why didn't you just say that?"

Maverick rolled his eyes and I smiled at the sibling back and forth. As an only child that was something I never got to experience. But watching Maverick with his siblings was endearing to me for some reason.

"Aight, chill. Fuck!" Maverick said, with a grin on his face. "I'll be there in ten."

He hung up the phone and looked at me.

"You have to go," I said.

"I have to go," he confirmed. "I'm sorry."

"Don't be!" I said, shaking my head. "What time should I get over there for the wedding?"

"I'll have a car come and pick you up," Maverick said.

"Mav. You don't have to do that," I insisted.

"I want to do it," he said. "Let me take care of you."

Those words made a warmth bloom in my chest.

"Okay," I acquiesced.

I watched as Maverick went to his closet and quickly returned with a garment bag slung over his shoulder. He sauntered back over to me and hooked his finger beneath my chin and lifted my face up to meet his gaze.

"Like I said earlier, make yourself at home with whatever you want. The fridge is fully stocked if you get hungry. Or if you want to soak in my tub and send me some more sexy ass pics," he teased, wiggling his eyebrows.

I shook my head and tried to playfully shove him away, but he grabbed my wrist and tugged, pulling my body hard against his before he dropped his mouth down on mine for a long, drugging kiss.

I had to be the one to break off the kiss and this time I really did push him away. Otherwise I was going to drag him to that big bed and make him late.

"Go," I urged him. "I'll see you later."

"See you later," Maverick said before he turned and left the room.

A few minutes later, I heard the garage door open and close back not long after. I went out to the porch from his bedroom and watched as his SUV drove away. He must have saw me because he honked his horn as he kept driving and then stuck his hand out the window and waved.

Smiling, I waved back before turning and going back into the bedroom.

How the hell had I ended up here? I pondered, as I shut the door behind me.

All I'd had planned for when I came to Noir Cove was to try and find my muse, my inspiration to write again.

But somehow I'd found that and so much more by meeting Maverick.

I thought back on the conversations we'd had over the last few days.

Maverick made me laugh, challenged me, made me think outside of the box, and inspired me.

Seems like Mrs. Lee was right about good dick being good inspiration, I thought with a grin.

The last few days with him had been some of the best days of my life and I knew I would cherish them forever.

I stood in Maverick's bedroom, staring at the Alaska King bed. A grin spread across my face as I ran and dove into the humongous bed. It felt like I'd landed on a cloud, I thought as I rolled onto my back and let out a long sigh.

I looked up at the sky through the skylight overhead and wondered to myself what would happen after I had to leave Umber Bluffs.

We'd only known each other for a short amount of time, but our connection felt so strong. And I knew it wasn't just me.

It feels like we've known each other for a lifetime.

I thought back on those words Maverick had said to me.

I'd absolutely felt the same way.

Maybe that's how love at first sight worked? When you meet someone and there was just something about that person that felt like you've met before, be it in this lifetime or a lifetime in the past. Like your souls have been intertwined forever. Like no matter what happens in life you're destined to be together.

Maybe that was the true secret to love at first sight.

I shook my head. What in the world was I thinking? Love?

Was I in love with Maverick?

I couldn't be!

Not this quickly.

But no matter how much I tried to deny it, I had to admit to the fact that it felt like he'd somehow already managed to capture a piece of my heart.

Chapter Ten

PEYTON

> MAV
>
> The car will be there in fifteen.
>
> Okay. I'm ready.

I looked at myself in the full-length mirror in Maverick's closet one last time before turning to head outside to wait for the car.

I felt amazing in the strapless burnt orange floor-length chiffon dress and I couldn't wait for Maverick to see me in it.

I'd FaceTimed Bianca to show off my dress and tell her about how I was extending my stay at Noir Cove in Umber Bluffs and she'd squealed with delight.

"Okay," she'd said. "I'm *so* happy that you've managed to get your writing groove back. But I'm also excited that you got your Stella groove back as well!"

I'd laughed as I watched her do a little shimmy dance into the phone.

"Seriously though, Pey," Bianca said. "You look so refreshed and happy and I love all of this for you!"

We chatted for a few more minutes before she had to quickly get off the phone thanks to what she called 'all day sickness'. I'd sent her my love and hung up so that she could run to the bathroom and I could finish getting ready.

Just as I was walking out of the house, a car pulled up and parked in the circular front driveway. I closed the door behind me and when I turned back towards the car, I smiled at the familiar face that suddenly appeared.

"Daniel!"

"Miss Baker," Daniel said as he opened the back door. "Hello again."

"Hello again," I replied as I slid into the back seat.

We chatted amicably on the drive. Daniel never once mentioned anything about me and Maverick or anything about the fact that he was picking me up from Maverick's place this time. The only thing he'd done was give me a knowing smirk when he first greeted me, but other than that he was respectful of our privacy.

"Here we are," Daniel said when we pulled up to the main lodge. "Enjoy the wedding."

"Thank you, Daniel," I said.

I went to grab the door handle but the door suddenly swung open and a hand reached in for me.

My body shivered when our hands connected and he helped me out of the backseat.

"What are you doing here?" I asked, my heart racing at the sight of Maverick.

He looked absolutely delectable in his tuxedo.

He just stood there, staring at me in awe.

"I couldn't wait to see you," he finally said. "And I'm

glad I came out here, because..." He shook his head and whispered, "*Wow*! You are absolutely breathtaking, Pey."

"Thank you," I said. "So are you."

"I can't stay for long," he said, holding his arm out to me. I hooked my arm around his and let him guide me into the lodge. "But I wanted to meet you and take you to your seat."

"I appreciate it since I don't really know anyone besides you and your siblings."

"I got you," he said with a wink.

We went through the lobby and took a turn that took us outside.

"Oh my goodness," I said, as I looked around at the outdoor area that had been transformed into a romantic paradise.

Rows and rows of chairs covered in flowers were on either side of the white carpet that had been rolled out to create an aisle that led to a flower covered arch that faced the lake.

"This is...so beautiful," I said, feeling my eyes get misty. "Sorry. Weddings make me all mushy."

"Don't apologize," Maverick said, smiling down at me. He caressed my cheek and then leaned down and pressed a sweet kiss to my lips. "I have to get back to the groom."

"Of course," I said. "Go! I'll be fine by myself."

Maverick gave my hand one final squeeze before letting it go and turning to head off. I watched him for a few minutes as he spoke to several people – fist bumping a few guys, hugging a few ladies – before he finally disappeared.

I turned and sat down in my seat, smiling at the woman next to me.

"How do you know the bride and groom?" she asked.

"Oh...ummm...through Maverick and Monica," I said.

"I see," she said. "That Maverick. He's quite the looker."

"You're not wrong about that," I said, smiling at her.

Thirty minutes later, the wedding started.

Maverick slowly came down the aisle with an older woman that I assumed was their grandmother. As he walked past my row, he locked eyes with me and winked.

His subtle flirting made me blush and I found it hard to focus on the rest of the bridal party coming down the aisle.

Eventually we all stood as it was time for Tatum to enter.

She looked absolutely stunning in her beautiful wedding dress. Her makeup and hair were flawless, but it was the look on her face that was captivating. Her eyes were clearly locked on to her groom as she walked down the aisle arm in arm with her father.

Tatum's eyes shimmered with unshed tears and love and when I looked up at Mason waiting for her beneath the archway, his eyes were filled with just as much love and there was a tear streaming down his cheek.

I smiled when I watched Maverick pass him a handkerchief and Mason gave his brother a discreet fist bump of thanks.

Tatum and her father stopped at the end of the aisle and the pastor asked who was giving Tatum away. A woman stood up and went to the other side of Tatum as her father announced, "Her mother and I do."

Tatum hugged and kissed both of her parents and then Tatum's father took her hand and placed it into Mason's hand before patting him on the shoulder.

The wedding ceremony was beautiful and I found myself dabbing my tears away during their vows. Every once in a while I would look over at Maverick and every time I did, I found him looking at me.

His gaze caused my stomach to flutter every single time. It made me dizzy with desire.

I'd been so caught up in our sensual stare down that I'd barely heard, "You may kiss the bride."

It was the clapping all around me that brought me out of my lusty haze. I joined in on the applause and watched as Tatum and Mason sealed their promise to love each other for eternity with a kiss.

"Ladies and gentlemen, Mr. and Mrs. Porter!" the pastor announced and everyone stood and cheered and clapped even louder.

Tatum and Mason led the way back down the aisle followed by their wedding party. Maverick came back down the aisle with his grandmother once again and our gazes briefly connected.

"Ladies and gentleman," the pastor spoke. "The reception will be in the Alora Atrium. So please feel free to head over there for the cocktail hour."

Everyone stood up and I followed the crowd over to the atrium. There were servers moving around the room offering glasses of champagne so I took one and then found a seat.

There wasn't assigned seating, so I sat down at a table by one of the large windows that had a view of the mountains. The sun was setting and it looked beautiful.

It reminded me of spending time with Maverick out on the lake at sunset. Then of course I thought about later on that night and how we'd spent it making love.

The soft music that had been playing suddenly switched to an upbeat song and the volume cranked up as the DJ's voice came through the speakers.

"Ladies and gentlemen…let's give a round of applause as our wedding party enters!"

Everyone clapped as one by one each member of the wedding entered.

"Now get up on your feet and welcome Mr. and Mrs. Porter!" the DJ shouted.

Everyone stood and cheered as Mason and Tatum entered the reception hall hand in hand. The cheers grew even louder when Mason spun Tatum into his arms, dipped her and gave her a long kiss.

I sat back down as Mason and Tatum began to stroll around the room, receiving hugs and congratulations from everyone.

I was sipping my wine when my gaze suddenly found Maverick. He was talking to two beautiful women, one I recognized as a bridesmaid. He looked my way and then back at them and shook his head.

After another minute, I watched as he rolled his eyes and turned to head my way with both women in tow.

"Unhand me woman!" he said to the bridesmaid. "You're digging your daggers into my arm." He turned his gaze back to me and smiled. "Hey!"

"Hey," I said. "The ceremony was beautiful."

"Yeah."

"Ahem," the bridesmaid who'd been clutching Maverick's arm said in a playfully loud tone before elbowing him in the side.

"Keep that shit up and I won't introduce y'all," Maverick threatened.

"Okay," she whisper-yelled. "I'm sorry, I'm sorry."

Maverick shook his head. "Peyton, these are my cousins Audrey and Jasmine."

Audrey, the bridesmaid, took a step forward. "We are *huge* fans of your books!" Audrey exclaimed.

"Oh! Really?" I asked as I stood. "Thank you. And it's nice to meet you both."

"Nice to meet you too," Jasmine said, smiling at me. "And please excuse our audacious ass cousin."

"It's fine!" I insisted.

"So we have a book club here in Umber Bluffs and I was wondering if you'd be interested in attending one of our meetings."

"Audrey!" Maverick said, annoyance on his face.

I placed a calming hand on his shoulder. "I would love to!" I said. "Get my contact information from Maverick and just let me know when and where and I will be there!"

"I told you she'd say yes!" Audrey said excitedly before pulling me into a hug. "Thank you!"

"No, thank you!" I said.

"Audrey owns the local coffee shop, Café Noir," Maverick explained.

"That's where we always hold our book club meetings," Audrey added.

"I will have to stop by before I head back to the city," I said.

"And Jas owns a local flower shop," Maverick said. "She actually did all of the floral arrangements for the wedding."

"You did a spectacular job," I gushed. "Everything was so gorgeous."

"Thank you!" Jasmine said. She hooked her arm into Audrey's. "It was so nice meeting you Peyton."

"It was nice meeting you too," I said, waving as they headed off.

I looked up at Maverick, who was staring down at me. It was the first time we'd kind of been alone since I'd first arrived for the wedding.

"Have I told you how amazing you look tonight?" he asked, taking a step closer to me.

"You have," I said, taking a step closer to him. "But I'll never get tired of hearing your compliments."

Maverick wrapped a hand around my waist and closed the last bit of distance between us by pulling me flush against his body.

"You look so fucking stunning," he murmured, lowering his mouth down towards mine.

Just as our lips were about to connect, someone called out Maverick's name.

"Fuck," he growled under his breath and then moved away. I instantly missed his closeness.

We turned to find the bride and groom heading our way. Tatum had changed out of her wedding dress into a much simpler dress for the reception but she looked just as beautiful in this dress as well.

"Peyton?" Tatum asked.

"That's me. Congratu–oh!"

Tatum pulled me in for a hug.

I looked over her shoulder to see Mason smiling at me.

"Hello again," I said.

"Hello again," Mason said. "In person for real this time."

"Mason and Maverick told me that you were the one who helped with our catering situation," Tatum said as she pulled out of the hug. "Thank you so much."

"You're very welcome," I said. "Cole is a great person and caterer."

"I heard my name over here."

I turned to find Cole and…

"Bee Bee!" I exclaimed.

"Surprise!" Bianca giggled as I rushed over to hug her.

"What are you doing here?" I asked.

"Cole needed a few extra hands to help cater the wedding so I offered," she said. "And since I was tagging along, we decided to just stay at Noir Cove for the entire weekend."

"That sounds wonderful."

I introduced Bianca to everyone and then Cole announced that the appetizers were ready.

"Why didn't you tell me you were here when I talked to you earlier?" I asked when Bianca and I were alone. "Were you even really sick earlier?"

"Nah, I just had to get off the phone so I could get to helping Cole prep. And I didn't tell you because I wanted to surprise you," Bianca said. Lowering her voice, she added, "And I wanted to see this Maverick Porter with my own two eyes in the flesh. Giiiiirl."

"I know, right?" I whispered.

"I saw y'all over here lookin' real cozy. And don't even get me started on how much y'all are oozing hotness."

I shook my head and smiled at her. "How are you feeling?"

"I feel good!" Bianca said.

"You look good."

"Well, let me get back there to help Cole in the kitchen," she said, pulling me in for another hug. "If I don't see you anymore, I'll catch up with you when you get back home."

"For sure. Love you."

"Love you back."

Maverick ended his conversation with his brother and sister-in-law and came back over to me.

"I've got a few more things I have to do as the best man, and then I'm all yours for the rest of the night," he said, taking my hand in his for a moment.

"I can't wait," I said.

Maverick lifted my hand and pressed a kiss to the back of it before letting it go.

I made my way over to grab some appetizers and then went back to my table.

The other people at my table were nice and we had a good time laughing and enjoying our food.

A little while after dinner was served, Maverick stood up. Several people clinked their knives against their glasses and the conversations around the room grew silent.

"Good evening everyone," he started. "I'm Mason's younger brother, Maverick. And also the best man. Thank you all for joining us in celebrating this…momentous occasion of Mason and Tatum's wedding."

Everyone clapped and once the applause died back down, Maverick continued his speech. "We've been friends with Tatum and her brother since we were kids. Mason and Tommy have been best friends since then and Tatum was always around, much to Tommy's annoyance."

There were a few light chuckles.

"As we grew up, it was clear that they always had feelings for one another. Although for quite a long while, their timing seemed to always be…off. But *thankfully* their timing finally aligned."

Somebody let out a loud whoop and Maverick smiled.

My heart clutched when I saw him start to speak again but had to take a moment to let out a deep fortifying breath.

"Our parents…" He stopped again and cleared his throat. I felt my eyes begin to water as I watched his siblings. Monica dabbed a tear away and Mason lowered his head as Tatum gently rubbed his back.

Finally, Maverick was able to continue. "Our parents were the epitome of black love. They were an inspiration for my siblings and me. They would have been so proud and happy for this moment. I know they are dressed in their best and already hitting the electric slide in Heaven."

He lifted his glass. "Mason, Tatum, we love you guys so much and we are so happy that you managed to find your way to one another. Your love is now also inspiration for us all. May you continue to laugh, love, and live out your days happily ever after. To Tatum and Mason."

Everyone chorused, "To Tatum and Mason!" and Mason stood and went to pull Maverick in for a strong, long brotherly hug.

When they finally pulled apart, Mason used the back of his hand to wipe his damp eyes and Tatum stood to embrace Maverick as well.

The rest of the speeches were lovely as well, but admittedly none of them held my attention the way Maverick's had.

Once the toasts were done, Tatum and Mason shared their first dance together as husband and wife. Tatum danced with her father next and finally, Mason danced with their grandmother, Doris.

Their dance was the most entertaining as they had a whole ass routine. We laughed and cheered as they moved and grooved on the dance floor. Miss Doris was in her late seventies but looked to be at least twenty years younger and still moved like someone in their twenties. I'd overheard someone say she'd been a dancer and owned a dance studio in Umber Bluffs. Miss Doris was giving Debbie Allen vibes and I was here for it as I clapped for them when they ended their dance.

I knew it had to be rough for Mason not to be able to do the mother of the groom dance with his mom, but his grandmother had been an amazing stand in and had made what could have been a sad moment something so much fun and full of joy.

Maverick introduced me to Doris after their dance and she was warm and welcoming and reminded me of Mrs.

Lee. She also told me she couldn't wait to start reading my books and that made me smile, especially since it made Maverick cringe.

They opened the dance floor up to everyone and Maverick immediately took me out there, and we danced until it was time for the bouquet and garter tosses.

I tried to sneak off, but Monica got a hold of me and dragged me back out there.

"If I have to be out here, so do you," she teased.

Tatum tossed it and even without trying to catch it, I still ended up with the bouquet.

I held the bouquet up and waved it overhead and I hurried off the dance floor.

All the single men crowded the floor next, and Mason flung the garter. One of their cousins ended up catching the garter.

He sauntered over to me, spinning the garter on his finger.

"You know, usually whoever catches the garter has to put it on the thigh of whomever caught the bouquet," he said, licking his lips.

"Yo Darryl…"

Darryl looked over his shoulder to find Maverick staring at him menacingly.

"Step the fuck off, cuz."

"Oh this you, fam?" Darryl asked, as he pointed at me.

"You know gotdamn well she's with me," Maverick nearly growled. "Move around."

"My bad, my bad," Darryl said, forcefully pressing the garter into Maverick's chest. "I was just fuckin' around."

Darryl left and I smiled up at Maverick.

"You looked like you were gonna clobber his face in."

"I was," Maverick said, shoving the garter into his

pocket. "That motherfucker always takes shit too damn far."

"Well," I said, sliding my hands up his chest in an attempt to calm him down. "I can handle myself just fine. But I appreciate you for stepping in so I didn't have to."

Maverick let out a little grunt and I raised up on my tiptoes to press a kiss to his lips.

I felt his body melt against mine, any last remnants of frustration disappearing as I continued to kiss him. He wrapped an arm around me as he deepened the kiss.

Not wanting to give the folks around us too much of a show, I pulled away.

"How much longer?" I whispered.

"Not much," he said. "They're about to cut the cake and Monica is already passing out the sparklers so we can send them off."

I nodded, staring up into his eyes that were filled with as much heat as I was feeling at the moment.

Although I'd had a wonderful time at the wedding and the reception, I was more than ready to get back to Maverick's house and rip that tuxedo off of his sexy body.

Tatum and Mason did the cake cutting ceremony and Maverick and I shared a slice.

Afterwards, we went back out to the dance floor for a little while longer. I had a great time line dancing with Miss Doris. And I loved watching Maverick get down with his fraternity brothers.

Soon Monica came by and handed us some sparklers and a lighter and we started to head outside where a limo was waiting to take Mason and Tatum off to the airport for the honeymoon trip. Maverick lit my sparkler first and then his, and a few minutes later we lifted them up into the air, creating a sparkly arch for them to run under.

Once again, Mason dipped Tatum and kissed her

deeply and I knew that picture was going to be one of the best ones taken of the night, with them surrounded by sparklers lighting the night sky with the moonlit mountains in the background.

They hurried through the sparkler arch, stopping to hug on Maverick, Monica and Doris and then made their way into the limo. Once they were gone, Maverick took my hand.

"I've got to tell the fam goodbye and then I'm all yours," he said.

"Okay," I said, liking the sound of him being all mine.

"Do you want to come with me or are you cool here?"

"I'm cool here," I said, smiling at him.

Maverick nodded and dropped a quick kiss on my lips before heading back into the atrium where everyone else was heading.

I stood watching from a distance as Maverick went around the reception hall speaking to his family. Just as Maverick was hugging his sister goodbye, something out of my peripheral caught my eye.

I tried not to roll my eyes when I saw Mav's cousin Darryl coming over to me.

"Miss Bouquet winner," he slurred, as he drunkenly swayed over to me. "Too bad Maverick's wack ass stole my damn garter."

I wanted to remind him that he'd actually given Maverick the garter, but instead I chose not to respond. I just stood there staring straight ahead.

I closed my eyes and balled up my fists when Darryl leaned in towards me, the smell of liquor on his breath making my stomach roil, as he said, "Maverick thinks he's big shit. All three of 'em think they are. Just cause they own this place. They always thought they was better than us. But Maverick ain't shit." He skimmed his fingers along the bare skin of my shoulder and I jerked away from him as he said, "You shouldn't be with his wack ass. Why don't you let me take you back to my place and show you what a *real* man can do?"

"You mean what a real *drunk* man can do?" I spat out, before trying to step around him to head to the atrium to find Maverick. "I'm sure you'd be great for a whole ass thirty seconds of thunder."

Darryl grabbed me by the wrist and painfully yanked me around to face him.

"What the fuck did you say, bitch?!" he spat out.

"Let me go," I said through clenched teeth, but he just squeezed my wrist even harder.

"Oh, so you one of them mouthin' off bitches," he said, leering at me. "I bet Maverick don't even know how to tame a wild bitch like you."

I tried to wrestle out of his grasp but the harder I fought, the tighter he held on.

"Let me go," I repeated.

Darryl pulled me closer against him, grabbing my face with his other hand and squeezing. "Oh yeah, I could tame your ass," he said into my ear. "And you'd love it too. You'd be beggin' me to—"

"The only thing I'd be beggin' for is for it to hurry up and be over," I angrily replied, shaking my face out of his hand.

My words seemed to set him off even more, the crazy look in his eyes intensifying.

My eyes went wide as I watched Darryl's free hand rear back and then start coming towards my face. I tensed and lifted my free hand to my face to try and block the slap that I couldn't avoid because I couldn't get away from him, but suddenly Maverick's booming voice echoed in the lobby as he roared out Darryl's name.

Darryl released me and started backing up as Maverick stalked over to him.

"You keep your fuckin' hands off of her," Maverick spit out as his fist connected with Darryl's jaw.

"What the fuck?" Darryl screeched. "We was just talkin', man!"

"You don't ever fuckin' learn," he growled as he grabbed Darryl by the lapels of his suit jacket. Maverick slammed Darryl against a pillar. "I told you earlier to step the fuck off. And I come out here to find you with your hands on my lady. About to fucking hit *my* lady?!"

"Get yo fuckin' hands off me, man," Darryl said as he tried to shove Maverick away. "Here come Maverick ol' knight in shining armor ass nigga. Your *lady* is a smart mouth bitch, and her ass needs to be put in her place."

Maverick was about to punch Darryl again when his grandmother shouted, "Maverick! Enough."

"Nah!" Maverick said as two of the Noir Cove security guards grabbed his arms and tried to hold him back. "I'm sick of Darryl and his bullshit. He always like this."

"I know," his grandmother said in a gentle tone. "But you've got to calm down, baby. You're making a scene. Remember where you're at."

Those words seemed to snap him out of his rage.

He shook the security guards off of him and straightened his tuxedo jacket.

"Escort him off my property," Maverick said before turning to walk away from him. He started walking away, grabbing my hand and pulling me along with him.

I could still see that he was angry, but was trying to reign it in, especially when Darryl yelled at Maverick, "Aye yo fuck you, Mav! Y'all ain't better than us just cause you own this lil resort. *Fuck you*! And fuck that bitch too!"

I squeezed Maverick's hand tighter when I felt him trying to turn back around and we kept walking away.

I looked over my shoulder just in time to see Miss Doris slapping the shit out of her grandson.

"That's why nobody likes inviting his ain't shit ass to events," I heard Maverick mumble under his breath as we continued walking to the truck.

"Hey," I said, planting my feet and stopping us when we were in the parking lot. I squeezed his hand and tugged it. "Maverick."

Maverick stopped and turned to look down at me.

I cupped his cheek. "Take a breath."

Maverick inhaled deeply and let out a long sigh.

"Again," I gently ordered, placing my other hand on his heart. I could feel it rapidly beating.

He did it again and I could see the tension begin to melt away.

He pulled me against his body and pressed his forehead against mine.

"I'm sorry," he said.

"Sorry for what?" I asked.

"I just…I hate you saw me like that." Maverick shook his head and tried to look away from me but I grabbed his face in my hands, forcing him to look at me.

"Saw you swooping in and protecting me? Defending my honor?" I asked. "That's all I saw. You have *nothing* to apologize for. I'm glad you showed up when you did."

"I am too. Things would have been a lot worse if I came out there and saw that he'd actually hit you."

I had no doubt that Maverick would have beat the shit out of his cousin if he'd saw that Darryl had actually hit me.

"How's your fist?" I asked, lifting his hand to inspect it.

His knuckles were a little bruised but they weren't too bad. I pressed a soft kiss against his knuckles.

"I'll be fine," Maverick insisted. He cupped my face, caressing my cheek with his thumb. "Are *you* okay?"

"I'm fine," I insisted.

"I'm sorry you had to experience my raggedy ass cousin."

I shrugged. "Families."

"Yeah."

"What's his problem anyway?" I asked once we were in Maverick's SUV and driving back to his house.

Maverick tsked. "Man, that nigga is basically holding on to a twenty-year old grudge," he grumbled.

"Seriously?" I asked. "What happened?"

"When we were teenagers, he was always in some kind of trouble," Maverick started. "His mom, my mom's sister, reached out to my parents and asked them to give him a summer job. Hoping it would teach him some discipline or…how to get his own head out of his ass or some shit. My dad agreed and gave him a job, and in Darryl's warped ass mind that just meant that he was gonna coast through the summer getting paid to do nothing since he was working at a business ran by his relatives. Well Pop's wasn't having any of that lazy ass shit, so he fired Darryl a week after he hired him. His entitled ass has been mad about it ever since and always likes to hem and holler about how we think they're better than them."

"Oh wow," I said when Maverick finished.

"Yeah," Maverick muttered. "And it's bullshit because that has *never* been the case. I always wanted us *all* to succeed, ya know? Did my best to try to make sure that we were all set. Even after all that shit when we were teens, I tried hiring him again after my parents died. And it was just the same bullshit. So, I fired him as well."

"You did the right thing," I said, reaching over to place my hand on top of his. "You can't always take everybody with you on your journey to success, not even if they're family."

"I know," Maverick said. He blew out a breath. "It's just always some kind of drama whenever he comes around."

"I see." Looking on the bright side of things, I pointed out, "At least he didn't make a scene until after the wedding and reception were pretty much over and Mason and Tatum had already taken off."

"Yeah," Maverick agreed as we pulled into his garage. He turned off the vehicle and just sat there for a moment, squeezing the steering wheel. "When I came out to get you and I saw you trying to get away from him and then saw him lifting his hand at you. I just…I fucking lost it, Pey."

"I know," I sighed. "But everything is okay now."

Maverick nodded and we sat in silence for a moment.

I ran my hand along his tense forearm, up to his shoulder and then took his chin and turned his face towards mine. I leaned over the console as I pulled his face down onto mine.

The kiss started off slow and gentle. But then Maverick leaned into it more, deepening the kiss as his hand cupped the back of my head.

"Let's go inside," I said against his lips.

Maverick nodded and hopped out of the SUV and came to open the door for me.

We went into the house, holding hands and went upstairs to his bedroom.

Maverick shut the door behind us and I walked over to the floor-to-ceiling window, admiring the beautiful view.

"I can't believe you get to look at this all the time," I whispered.

My eyes fluttered closed when I felt Maverick wrap a strong arm around my waist. My head tilted to the side as he pressed a kiss against my neck.

His other hand glided down the side of my body, pausing momentarily at the swell of my hip before moving further down to where the long split in my dress began.

"Do you know how hard I had to fight the urge all night to snatch your fine ass up, take you to my office and fuck the shit out of you?" he murmured into my ear as his hand dipped past the slit in my dress to caress my bare thigh.

"I think I have an idea of just how hard," I said, pressing my ass against his erection.

His hand moved from my thigh over to my thong. His fingers danced along the elastic band, and I thrusted my hips forward, eager to feel him touch me. My pussy was aching and drenched with desire.

I nearly whimpered when he moved his hand from under my dress. Maverick spun me around and crushed his lips against mine as he pressed me up against the window. I rocked my hips against his as I grabbed his jacket and shoved it off of his shoulders. Once his arms were free, he lifted my arms overhead, locking them in place with one of his big strong hands.

His other hand found the zipper on the side of my dress and tugged it down. My dress pooled to my feet as Maverick's mouth moved down my body, kissing the tops of my bountiful breasts that were being held up in my strapless lace bra.

I let out a moan when Maverick unhooked my bra and captured one of my hard nipples into his mouth.

"Mav," I rasped, pushing my breast further into his mouth. His teeth sank into the turgid peak before his tongue swirled around it to soothe that sting. He kissed his way over to the other breast, showering it with the same attention he'd given to the first one, before he stood tall and finally released my arms from overhead.

The moonlight illuminated his dark, handsome face as he studied me with a look in his eyes I couldn't quite read.

There was something on his mind.

"What is it?" I finally asked.

"This…thing between us," Maverick said as he caressed my face. "I don't want it to end when you leave Noir Cove."

"You don't?" I asked, my heart starting to race even faster.

"No," Maverick said, shaking his head. "I…These last few days with you have been amazing. I want more of this. I want more of you."

My eyes drifted closed as he pressed a kiss on the sensitive spot right behind my ear and whispered, "I want you to be mine, Peyton."

I opened them back up when I felt Maverick had pulled away to look down at me again.

I remembered the way he'd possessively referred to me as his lady more than once during the incident with Darryl.

It felt good hearing him say that. It felt right.

"I want the same thing," I said. "I want you–"

Maverick crushed his lips against mine and picked me up. I wrapped my legs around his waist as he carried me over to the bed.

"You've got on way too many clothes," I said after he laid me in the middle of the huge bed.

I sat up and watched as he reached up and tugged on his tie to loosen and then remove it. He never took his eyes off of me as he stripped. My heart pounded with each button he undid.

I crawled towards him standing at the edge of the bed as he unbuckled his belt and then undid his pants. He pulled them down along with his underwear and as soon as his dick sprang free, I took it into my hands and wrapped my mouth around it.

"Pey," Maverick wheezed. "Fuuuuck!"

I went to work sucking his dick further into my mouth. I moved my hands in slow strokes that I could tell was driving him crazy by the way he was moaning.

Maverick buried his hand in my hair, cradling the back of my head as he rolled his hips.

"That's it, baby," he said through gritted teeth. "This dick belongs to you. Throat that shit."

Hearing him say that his dick belonged to me turned me on even more. I pulled away until just the tip was around my lips and swirled my tongue around the head, causing Maverick to let out a hiss. I licked the entire length from the base all the way up the shaft before pulling him back into my mouth.

"Shit!" Maverick groaned, wrapping his fingers around the coils in my hair as he began to thrust his hips. "That shit feels so good."

My head bobbed back and forth and I lifted my gaze up to his as I took him deeper and deeper down my throat, causing my eyes to water. Maverick's eyes were filled with heat and lust as he watched me masterfully suck his dick. His moans mixed with the slurping sounds coming from my mouth as saliva began to drizzle down my chin.

My hands and mouth moved in tandem on his dick and soon he was tugging on my hair, trying to pull me off of him.

"Pey…Peyton," he grunted as his eyes squeezed shut and his head fell back. "Baby, I'm about to…"

He tried to pull away again, but I stayed right where I

was as I suctioned my mouth around him even harder and began to jack him off even faster.

Maverick let out a string of obscenities as he filled my mouth, his entire body tensing.

I finally released him from my mouth and watched as he stood there, swaying slightly, breathing heavily.

I wiped my mouth with the back of my hand feeling satisfied that I'd been able to drive him absolutely wild with my mouth.

"I think you just sucked my fucking soul out through my dick," he said, when he was finally able to speak again.

"Sorry…?" I teased, watching Maverick kick off his shoes, socks and step out of his pants.

"Don't you dare fucking apologize. You can have it," he said as he crawled into the bed and on top of me. He caged my head in with his big strong arms. "You can have whatever the fuck you want from me, gorgeous."

Can I have your heart?

That felt like it came from out of nowhere.

"What's wrong?" Maverick asked, making me realize I must have given away on my face that my last thought had startled me a bit.

It was crazy that after just a few days, I was having thoughts like this about this man. But here I was. And he'd already admitted that he wanted me to be his and I'd told him I wanted him as well. The heart was part of that package deal, wasn't it?

I smiled up at him and shook my head.

"Nothing is wrong," I said, reaching up to stroke his face.

He studied me for another moment and then leaned down to kiss my lips. It was a slow and worshipful kiss that had my entire body vibrating with desire.

When I felt the tip of his dick, pressing against the seat of my panties, I wantonly lifted my hips.

Maverick's mouth moved to pepper kisses along my jaw, down my neck and across my collarbone. My body writhed beneath his as he continued his journey with his mouth further down my body to my breasts, massaging them both as he swirled his tongue around one areola and then the other.

He pressed a kiss to my belly before finally hooking his thumbs into the waistband of my thong. My body squirmed as he placed kisses on my thighs while peeling my panties off.

He finally removed my underwear completely and placed a kiss on my ankle.

"We're gonna keep these on for now," he said, referring to my stiletto heels.

He climbed his way back up my body, kissing, biting and nibbling on my skin, setting my insides on fire.

"Mav," I breathed, my breaths coming out in short bursts. I spread my legs when I felt his hand graze my inner thigh.

"You're so wet," Maverick murmured into my ear as he slid two fingers up and down my slit. He sank them between my slick folds as he asked, "Is this all for me, baby?"

"Yessss," I moaned. "It's all for you. It's all yours."

He let out a low growl before crushing his lips against mine. Our tongues tangled wildly as his fingers pumped in and out of me.

"I love the scent of your pussy in the air," he said after tearing his mouth away from mine. "That shit drives me crazy. *You* drive me crazy."

"I need to feel you inside of me," I damn near begged.

Maverick removed his hand from my pussy and

slammed his dick inside of me, causing me to cry out at the mixture of pain and pleasure.

He stayed there for a moment unmoving, buried deep inside of my pussy. He sat up and slowly slid out and then slowly dove back in, grinding his hips against mine when he was in as deeply as he could go.

He did it again…and again…and again…

Sliding out until just the tip was in, diving back in inch by delicious inch.

And then he slid his hands down my legs until he reached my feet and grabbed both of my stiletto heels and pushed my knees up to my ears as his slow and gentle strokes turned into harder, rougher and faster thrusts.

"Maverick!" I cried out as he rammed his dick inside of me over and over.

"You take this dick so fuckin' good, baby," he said, releasing one of my heels and wrapping his hand around my neck. "Fuck! You take this dick so good."

He gave my neck a gentle squeeze and it made me even wetter.

"That's it," Maverick grunted. "Cream all over my dick."

He commanded my body with his words and ministrations.

"Oh shit," I moaned. "*Yes yes yes…*"

I was on the verge of coming. My orgasm was building, and my body began to tremble.

Maverick suddenly released me and pulled out of me. He grabbed one of my ankles and tugged.

"Flip over," he ordered, and I quickly switched positions so that I was on my hands and knees.

He entered me from behind with a powerful thrust and smacked my ass causing me to let out a loud moan.

"Oh, you like that shit, huh?" Maverick asked,

smacking my ass again. "Yeah, you like that shit. Every time I smack this big sexy ass, you get even wetter on this dick."

He gave my ass one last smack and then gripped my hips as he went to work fucking me from behind.

I met him thrust for thrust as I threw my ass back against his pelvis, the sound of our bodies colliding over and over reverberating around the room.

My fists gripped the sheets as my body began to convulse.

Pleasure ripped through me as Maverick's fingers dug into my hips.

"Maverick!" I screamed as I came unglued, my orgasm shooting me into the stratosphere. "Don't stop! Don't ever stop!"

"Shit! Peyton," Maverick grunted as my pussy walls clenched around his dick.

He let out a feral roar as he pistoned in and out of me over and over before his entire body tensed.

He pulled out of me, and I felt the warms spurts of his cum coating my back.

I collapsed onto the bed, utterly spent but completely satiated.

I felt a shift in the bed and a moment later I heard the bathroom light turn on followed by the water running in the bathroom.

A couple minutes later, I felt a dip in the bed again as Maverick climbed back into it.

I let out a sleepy moan when I felt him wipe my back clean with a warm towel.

"I'm sorry, I was so fucking keyed up and eager to get inside of you that I forgot about protection," Maverick said quietly.

"I have an IUD," I muttered into a pillow. "And I got tested recently, all is well down there."

"Same here," Maverick said. "So what you're telling me is next time I ain't gotta pull out of that spectacular pussy of yours."

"No," I chuckled. "I suppose you don't have to."

"Duly noted."

He left the bed again and when he came back, he gave my hips a gentle tap. I lifted them up so that he could pull the covers from underneath me, so that we could get beneath them.

Once we were settled in, Maverick wrapped his arms around my waist and pulled me closer against his body.

"Pey?" he said into my ear.

"Hmm?" I sleepily replied.

He kissed my bare shoulder and I snuggled my ass even more against him.

"I meant what I said earlier," he whispered into the dark room.

"About what?"

"About not wanting for this thing between us to end after you leave," he said. "About you being mine."

"I know you meant it," I said, yawning. "I meant it too."

"Good," he said.

And then we finally drifted off to sleep.

Chapter Eleven

MAVERICK

My eyes slowly slid open, and I was greeted by the early morning light of the sky before the sun's ascent beaming through my skylight overhead. Memories of the night before came flooding back to the forefront of my mind as I took a long stretch. I inhaled deeply taking in Peyton's hypnotic scent that was now imbedded into my sheets and pillows.

Making love with Peyton had been out of this world. From the moment that she'd arrived at the venue for the wedding, I couldn't keep my eyes off of her. Even through the wedding when I was supposed to be focusing on the ceremony, more often than not, I'd end up just staring at her beautiful ass sitting in the crowd, counting down the hours until I could get her alone.

I'd been so damn distracted by her that the pastor had to clear his throat and call out my name to get my attention when it was time for me to present the rings I'd been responsible for holding on to during the ceremony.

I'd been completely serious when I told her that I'd considered sneaking off with her to my office to fuck her.

That's how much I craved her body.

But it had definitely been worth the wait, because when we finally got back to my house our lovemaking had been combustible. Each time was even better than the time before, I thought to myself as I rolled over to my side. I quickly sat up when I realized the other side of the bed was empty. My brows burrowed in confusion when I realized Peyton was nowhere to be seen in the room. I looked over to the bathroom and saw the door was open and the light was off.

It wasn't like she'd taken off since all of her stuff was still here, I thought as I continued looking around the room. I got out of bed and went over to look out the windows that faced the second story porch and saw Peyton sitting out there in one of the chairs, her back facing me.

I turned and went to my closet and grabbed a pair of pajama pants and threw on a shirt before heading outside to join her. I shivered when I was greeted by the coolness of the morning.

I stood there smiling at how adorable she looked – wrapped in a blanket, her hair up in a messy bun, big ass glasses on her face which was contorted in concentration as her fingers furiously flew across her wireless keyboard. From beneath her blanket, I could see that she was wearing my button-down shirt from last night.

That was a sight I could get used to. This whole situation was one I could get used to.

That idea caused a feeling of warmth to bloom in my belly.

I'd confessed to her the night before that I wanted her to be mine. And if moments like this were included then I was ready.

It felt good…It felt right.

I thought about my parents and the many times they'd shared their love story.

My father always told us that he'd known from the moment he first met our mother that he knew that she was the woman that he'd spend the rest of his life with.

I'd never understood how that was possible.

Until I met Peyton.

Our physical connection was potent. But the other connections we were already creating were wonderful as well.

She was intelligent and funny and sexy as hell.

I loved the way we could talk for hours about everything and nothing. I loved learning what made her mind tick, her likes, her dislikes.

It had only been days, but I loved everything about this woman.

I wasn't about to go around throwing that 'L' word around to Peyton yet, because I didn't want to scare her off. But I knew…the feelings I had for this woman were real and strong.

I knew we still had so much to learn about one another, but I knew I was going to enjoy every moment of it.

After taking another minute to just stand in awe of her beauty, I slowly made my way over to her. When she sensed my presence, she looked up at me and smiled.

"Up and at it already, I see?" I said, stopping right in front of her.

"Yep!" she said, stretching her arms overhead. "Good morning."

I leaned down and grabbed her chin between my fingers, tipping it up so I could place a kiss on her lips. "Good morning. Why the hell are you out here? It's chilly as fuck!"

Just like the evenings, because we were right by the water the mornings tended to be on the cooler side.

Peyton held up her keyboard which had the look of an old school type writer.

"My baby can get a little loud," she admitted.

"Like her owner," I teased, earning me a playful shove.

"*Anyway*, I didn't want the clickety clacking of my keyboard to wake you, so I came out here to write."

"You know you could have just gone down to my office," I reminded her as I walked over to the small fire pit and threw a couple of logs into it.

"I know," she said as I lit the fire and then turned back to face her. "But I've been enjoying writing while watching the sunrise."

"And how has writing this morning been going?" I asked, slipping into the large chair behind her, straddling my legs on the outsides of the chair. I wrapped my arms around her waist and pulled her body against mine as I buried my face into her neck.

"It's…going…well," she breathed as I peppered kisses on her soft skin. "I woke up *filled* with inspiration."

"Is that right?" I asked, peeling the blanket down, and pushing my shirt off of her shoulder so I could kiss her bare skin.

"Mm hmm," she sighed.

"I got some…inspiration I can fill you with right now," I muttered as I slipped my hand beneath the shirt and cupped her full breasts.

Peyton's head lolled back to rest on my shoulder and I kissed her exposed neck. She arched her body causing her breast to press harder against my hand and her ass ground into my burgeoning erection.

I squeezed her breasts as I continued kissing her neck. I

pinched and rolled her nipples between my fingers, eliciting a sexy little moan from her.

I moved one of my hands down her body and groaned when I reached the apex of her thighs and discovered that she wasn't wearing any panties.

"Maverick," she whispered as I slid a finger inside of her.

"Have you saved your work?" I asked into her ear as I pumped my finger in her pussy.

When she nodded, I grabbed her tablet and keyboard and moved them to the table next to the chair and dipped another finger inside of Peyton.

"Fuck," she said as she rocked her hips.

I grabbed her face and tilted her head so that I could kiss her. I slid my tongue along the seam of her mouth and she opened her mouth and began sucking on my tongue.

I bit down on her plump lower lip before pulling it into my mouth, as I sank my fingers deeper inside of her.

"I love feeling this tight pussy clench around my fingers…and my tongue…and my dick," I murmured into Peyton's ear. "I think I'm addicted to you."

"I'm addicted to you too…" she replied as she kept rolling her hips against my lap, making my dick even harder. "That feels so good."

"You're always so fucking wet," I groaned. I pulled my fingers out of her and held them up to her face. "Look how wet you always get for me."

I sucked in a ragged breath when she wrapped her pretty lips around my fingers and sucked her essence off of each digit.

That shit threw me into a ravenous frenzy. I grabbed her legs, spun her body around so that she was facing me and crushed my lips against hers. Tasting her sweet pussy on her tongue was intoxicating.

My dick was so fucking hard and the need to bury myself deep inside of her was damn near bordering on desperation.

Especially when Peyton cupped my shit in her hand and squeezed it.

"I want to ride it," she said against my lips, as she reached into my pants and pulled it out.

"I told you last night," I said, groaning when she squeezed me even harder. "You can have whatever the fuck you want, baby."

I lifted my hips to push my pajama pants off and then sat back in the chair.

"Come ride this dick," I said as it twitched in anticipation.

Peyton straddled my lap and gave my dick another squeeze before lining it up with her opening. She sank down a little bit and then rose back up off of it. A moment later she sank down deeper and stayed there for a moment, catching her breath as her body stretched to accommodate me.

Soon she was moving up and down on me at an unhurried pace. The feel of her pussy wrapped around my dick with no barrier felt out of this world. Needing to see every inch of her body, I grabbed my shirt and ripped it off her body, sending buttons flying everywhere.

"You just ruined a perfectly good shirt," she breathed as she continued riding my dick. She tried to smile and laugh, but her face contorted lasciviously and she let out a moan instead.

"Fuck that shirt," I growled as I slid one of my hands up her beautiful body until I reached her neck.

She wrapped her hand around my wrist and let out a moan when I gave her neck a squeeze.

"Maverick," she sighed as she ground down even

harder on my dick, finding a spot that seemed to feel good to her. "Mmm shit."

"That's it, baby," I said through gritted teeth, squeezing her neck again. "You're riding the shit out of this dick. Fuck."

"Mmm," she moaned again as she licked her lips.

My senses felt heightened as we continued to passionately make love outside.

Her moans mixed with the sound of her gushy pussy and the crackling of the fire filled the morning air and it was all music to my ears.

The flames illuminated her beautiful brown skin giving her an ethereal glow as she tossed her head back and started riding me harder and faster. Her titties danced in my face as she wildly bounced on my dick and unable to resist a moment longer, I pulled one into my mouth and sucked her hard nipple.

The feel of her soft fingers on my skin made my body sizzle.

And the scent of our sex in the air made my head spin.

"*Mav!*" Peyton whispered.

"Don't get all quiet now just cause we're outside," I growled, digging my fingers into her supple thighs. "Ain't nobody out here 'cept for you and me, baby. So let me hear you. Let me hear how good this shit is to you."

I lifted my hips in a powerful thrust and this time she wasn't timid about making her pleasure known.

"Whose pussy does this belong to?" I demanded to know.

"You," she murmured.

"What?" I asked, smacking her ass.

"You!" she cried out louder. "This pussy belongs to you."

"That's how I like to hear it," I said, giving her ass

another spank before I rubbed it to soothe the sting. "This pussy belongs to me. *You* belong to me."

"Yes…*yes*…*YES!*" Peyton exclaimed.

Her screams of passion echoed in the air as she climaxed, her walls clenching around my dick so hard that I found myself orgasming right along with her. My head fell back as I let out a primal roar, tightly wrapping my arms around her waist and holding her in place so that my dick rested in that sweet spot at the back of her pussy as I filled her up with my cum.

"Gotdammit," I breathed a moment later when my ears stopped ringing and my eyes were able to focus again.

I swung my legs to one side of the chair and stood with Peyton in my arms, my dick still buried inside of her and walked back into the bedroom.

I carried her all the way to the bathroom and to the shower, where I finally pulled out of her and put her down onto her feet.

I started the shower and we took a long, languid shower where we washed each other and stole sweet kisses.

Once we were clean, I gave her some of my sweatpants and an old shirt to put on and we got dressed and went down to the kitchen, where I made breakfast.

"Are you sure I can't help with anything?" Peyton asked, as I went to the fridge.

"Positive," I assured her as I pulled food out of the fridge and placed it on the island.

I set everything down and noticed the blueprints I'd forgotten to put away.

"What's this?" Peyton asked and then looked up at me. "May I?"

"Of course," I said. I went around to join her on the other side of the island. "They're blueprints for the next phase of Noir Cove and leveling up our glamping experience."

"Treehouses?" she murmured before looking up at me with bright eyes. "That sounds so cool."

"Think so?" I asked as I took the blueprints and rolled them up.

"Absolutely!"

I went to put them away in my office and when I came back, Peyton was staring at me, with a bright smile on her face.

"Your plans look amazing, Mav."

"Thank you," I said. I went back to spreading everything out to prep for breakfast. "I'm actually pretty excited about it. The first one is pretty much done. If we get good enough feedback from it we will add a few more."

"I can't wait to see it," Peyton said.

"Would you like to see it later on today?"

"Seriously?" she asked, genuinely interested.

"Yeah. We can drive out there later," I said. "I'd love to get your feedback. From a creative perspective."

"I'd love to," she said.

"Cool. We'll go later on."

It was honestly just another stall tactic to keep her around for just a bit longer. I knew I couldn't keep her here forever – not yet anyway – but any excuse to prolong our time together I was going to take advantage of it.

I turned on some music and we fell into a companionable silence as I made breakfast and she got back to working on her book.

"Done," I said about an hour later as I plated the last of the pancakes.

"Me too," Peyton said, giddily.

I raised an eyebrow as I looked at the smile of pride on her face.

"You mean…like *done* done?" I asked.

Peyton spun her tablet around to show me her document.

The words "The End" were on her screen.

"You finished!" I said, truly happy for her and proud of her. I rushed around the island and scooped her up into my arms and spun her around. "Congratulations!"

"Thank you!" she said, hugging my neck tightly.

I felt a bit of alarm when I sat her back down and realized her eyes were filled with tears.

"What's wrong?" I asked immediately, palming her face in my hands.

Peyton shook her head. "Nothing," she said. "I promise these are happy tears."

I nodded as I wiped them away from her cheeks.

She blew out a breath. "Sorry."

"You don't ever have to apologize for feeling your feelings around me," I informed her. "I just wanted to know how I could help fix things if they were anything other than happy tears."

"Thank you," she said. "And not just for that. Thank you for everything you've done for me over the last few days. You truly helped me find my muse."

I pressed my hand to her heart. "She was here the entire time," I said.

"I know. I just…I needed the reminder. So thank you for that. The last few days with you have been wonderful."

"They have been," I agreed. "And I can't wait to see what the future holds for us."

"I can't wait either," Peyton said.

I lowered my head and planted her lips with a sweet kiss.

"Come on," I said, finally managing to pull away from her addictive lips. I smacked her on the ass and pulled her chair out for her. "We've got some celebrating to do."

I grabbed a bottle of champagne out of the fridge and popped the cork, causing Peyton to burst out giggling as I turned her plain ol' orange juice into a mimosa.

"To finishing what I know will be another bestseller," I said, holding my glass up to hers.

Her face bloomed into the most beautiful of smiles. "Mav," she whispered. My name falling off those sweet lips was music to my ears that I knew I'd never grow tired of hearing.

"Cheers…to you, Pey," I said.

"Cheers…To *us*," Peyton added.

Those two simple words held so much promise that it made my heart swell.

"To us," I said.

We toasted to the future success of her newly completed book as well as the start of what I knew was going to be a beautiful relationship.

We enjoyed our first of many breakfasts together and then I took her back upstairs and back to my bed.

Where I filled her up with even more inspiration.

The End

Thank you!

Thank you so much for reading Wanderlust! I hope you enjoyed it! Please consider leaving a review on amazon, or messaging me your review to use it for promotional purposes!

You can email me your review at terussnovels@gmail.com.

About the Author

Té Russ is a contemporary romance author who focuses on stories centered around black love. With over 50 projects under her belt, she continues to bring soulful tales to life. In addition to writing, Té is also a certified aerial yoga instructor and a certified yoga instructor. She enjoys spending her free time with her family, baking, crocheting or reading.

Also by Té Russ

Standalone

Love by the Books

A Dash of Love (A Sweet Rapids Novella)

Santa Baby (A Sexy Holiday Short)

Runaway Love

Gingerbread Wishes (A Sexy Holiday Short)

Live at Five: A Té Russ Short

Dancing Through the Snow (A Sexy Holiday Short)

Birthday Sex (A Sexy Short by Té Russ)

Summer Fling

Falling For You

Grounded for Christmas (A Sexy Holiday Short)

Midnight Stroke (A Sexy Holiday Short)

A Scoop of Love (A Sweet Rapids Novella)

Lust at First Sight

Wicked (A Sexy Halloween Short)

Snowbound (An Umber Bluffs Story)

When in Rome

All I Want For Christmas

In the Key of Love

Rooted in Love (A Sweet Rapids Story)

There Goes the Bride

The Christmas Auction

Wanderlust

McAllister Friends

Dream Lover

Taking Chances

Always You

McAllister Family Series

After the Storm

Just One Kiss

Perfection

Love After War

Just One Night

Just Once Touch

Reckless Love (A McAllister Family/McAllister Security Crossover)

The Coalton, Texas Novella Series

Homecoming

Sanctuary

Reawakening

Destined

Irresistible

Four Seasons of Love Series

A Spring Affair
Sultry Summer Nights
Autumn Kisses
A Winter Rendezvous

In the Line of Love Series

Let Me Love You
Love's Taken Over

In the Line of Love: Fire & Rescue

Piece of My Love

The Nobles of Sweet Rapids

Noble Love
Noble Surrender
Noble Redemption
Noble Seduction

McAllister Security

Reckless Love (A McAllister Family/McAllister Security Crossover)
Dangerous Love
Vigilant Love
Resilient Love

Lessons in Love: A Series Collaboration with Nicole Falls and Bailey West

Acting on Love

The Wild Knights

Falling for a Knight
Claimed by a Knight
Seduced by a Knight

RAW: A Valentine's Short: A Series Collaboration with Danielle Allen and Bailey West

An Unexpected Valentine

RAW: VOL II: A Series Collaboration with Danielle Allen and Bailey West

Encore

Keep in Touch!

Facebook: www.facebook.com/TeRussNovels & www.facebook.com/TeRussAuthor
Twitter: www.twitter.com/TeRussNovels
Blog: www.terussnovels.blogspot.com
Email: terussnovels@gmail.com

Join my Facebook groups Té's Place for exclusive content and Spoiler Alert! when you wanna chat about the books in real time!

Copyright © 2024 by Té Russ

Wanderlust

All rights reserved.

No part of this book may be reproduced in any form or by any electronic or mechanical means, including information storage and retrieval systems, without written permission from the author, except for the use of brief quotations in a book review.

Made in the USA
Columbia, SC
08 June 2025